MEMOIRS
OF A
MILITARY
Diva

MEMOIRS
OF A
MILITARY
Diva

Lady Jay

iUniverse, Inc.
Bloomington

Memoirs of a Military Diva

iUniverse books may be ordered through booksellers or by contacting:

iUniverse
1663 Liberty Drive
Bloomington, IN 47403
www.iuniverse.com
1-800-Authors (1-800-288-4677)

ISBN: 978-1-4620-5079-6 (sc)
ISBN: 978-1-4620-5081-9 (hc)
ISBN: 978-1-4620-5080-2 (ebk)

Printed in the United States of America

iUniverse rev. date: 03/21/2012

Contents

Author's Note

This novel is a work of fiction. Characters, places, incidents, and names are either the product of the author's imagination or used fictitiously. Any resemblance to actual events or persons living or dead is entirely coincidental and not the intent of the author. I have chosen to refer to my book as a "memoir" because I wanted to share some of my personal experiences through the lives of the four main characters. Some of the situations have been exaggerated for entertainment purposes.

This book is dedicated to my mother. Thank you for everything. I couldn't have made it this far without you! You are truly a military diva!

PROLOGUE

He was a monster! Why am I paying the price for his scandal? thought Lisa while she walked slowly through the courtroom's double doors. The judge sat before her, waiting for her to be seated. It had been over two years, and after all the drama, it was all coming to an end. Her divorce was finally here. She sat less than six feet away from Brian, who refused to look in her direction. He knew he had broken her heart, but she needed him to see her tear-soaked face and truly comprehend her pain. His six-foot-tall, built frame stood proudly at the podium directly in front of the judge, and he was ready to strip from Lisa everything she'd worked so hard for. The clever fellow even had the audacity to wear his uniform. He was presenting himself as a patriotic American who spent four months raising a child on his own while the mother ran wild overseas. The judge would truly see what kind of woman Lisa Collier was.

The judge cleared his throat and then proceeded with the hearing. Every ounce of pain she'd ever felt throughout her marriage was sitting in the pit of her stomach. Brian and Lisa were destined to be together since the first moment she stepped foot on Dillan Air Force Base in Delaware. The relationship had had its ups and downs, but despite all the warning signs, they had pursued a marriage that was destined to fail. Thoughts of the past ran through her mind like a dramatic soap opera on replay. *Why is this happening?* Lisa knew she wasn't a very good spouse, but neither was he. They both had their problems, but she was more than willing to work it out as long as it was just the two of them. Instead, he ran off to another woman. She ran her hands through her hair and began to laugh at herself for crying. After all, she should be happy the marriage that nearly destroyed her life was coming to an end.

"All right, Lisa, it's time to pull yourself together," she mumbled while Brian tore her down word by word. "I must be cursed," she joked as she sat back in her chair, trying to take her mind off of Brian's rambling. He exposed every scandalous detail he could, hoping to convince the judge that Lisa was an unfit mother. Everything inside of her wanted to choke him until his last breath. She exhaled as long as she could. Her lawyer tapped her on the shoulder, shaking his head.

"Just remain calm. We'll get him," he warned. She nodded.

She focused her eyes on the American flag hanging in the corner of the tiny room. It symbolized freedom and pride, two things she recalled having when she first joined the military. Those were the days she remembered quite clearly. As a teenager coming out of high school, the military represented a newfound freedom. There was no more listening to Mother's rules. It was all about her. Then she did what most women do: she fell in love with the wrong man. Now she was paying the price.

CHAPTER 1

The Last Day of Basic Training

August 30, 2002

Straight out of air force basic training, Lisa Collier could not wait to leave Lackland Air Force Base in Texas. She was told at the military entrance processing station in Baltimore, Maryland, her job was going to be administration. Once graduation was over, she would run for the nearest bus and begin her next training in the beautiful state of Mississippi. After six weeks in hell—seven, including the infamous "zero" week consisting of nothing but paperwork and shots—she wasn't looking back. Her plan was to enter her new career field, just like her mother. When she stepped into out processing, she was led to the back office, where two sergeants sat at a desk opposite of each other. The small office was decorated with training certificates and pictures of spouses and children.

"Sit down, trainee," the bald man said. After enduring weeks of physical and mental training, she had earned the right to be called "airman," but arguing with a noncommissioned officer would have been a mistake. He was dressed in his crisp Class-A uniform, with enough cologne to fill the entire room. Judging by his demeanor, she could tell he was definitely cocky and proud. She didn't know if it was his cologne or his deep baritone voice that made the hair on her arms stand up. It was funny what

1

being enclosed in a dormitory of sixty-plus women could do to a girl. After all that estrogen, a little testosterone from almost anywhere was a breath of fresh air. He turned in her direction while she sat up straight and expressionless.

"Unfortunately, since there is minimum manning in the supply career field, you have been moved. You'll begin technical training with the 345th Training Squadron here in Lackland on Monday."

He handed her a folder and pointed to the door. As a new airman should, she kept her military bearing and rose to her feet. She wanted to jump across the table and claw his eyes out. How dare he ask her to stay here for another couple months! Basic training was bad enough, but to attend career training in Lackland was just cruel. She marched out the door to sit with the rest of the women. Lisa waited for a few people to pass and then took her seat next to her fellow basic training buddy, Denise.

"You mean to tell me I just signed my life away for four years and I'm not getting the job I want?" she whispered to the Denise.

Out of all the women in the flight, Denise was Lisa's wingman, the only one she could trust. Wingmen's duties included looking out for one another and encouraging each other through the tough times in training. No matter what, they always had each other's back. You needed that kind of comfort and stability in order to keep your sanity. The military training instructors were there to tear you down, and that is exactly what they did every chance they got, regardless of how quiet, clean, or well mannered you tried to be. The purpose was to break you down to nothing and then build you back to something. Both Lisa and Denise earned the position of being called element leaders; this meant they were in charge of six to ten women. If one failed a PT test, inspection, or just couldn't cut it, you would be sure the element leaders felt the wrath. In other words, they had to be babysitters so these women could pass, as if they held some kind of magic key to get through basic training. They were trainees themselves and just as clueless to the system. It was also a way for the drill instructors, famously known as "MTI's," to keep an extra eye on the flight when they were away. No one volunteers; it could be an honor or a nightmare. In most cases, it was a nightmare.

"Yeah, well, they assigned me to be a paramedic, and I'm squeamish." Denise sat shaking her head. "It's going to suck for those patients."

"Flight, head back to the dorms and get in gear. You have graduation rehearsal at fifteen hundred hours," Master Sergeant Miller screamed after the last trainee stepped out of the out processing line. He wore an air force blue campaign hat, heavily ironed battle dress uniform (BDU), and highly polished boots. The blue rope draped across his head gear indicated he was among the top 10 percent of his rank. Sergeant Miller was tough when it came to his flight, and he tolerated nothing but excellence.

"Oh, shut up," Lisa mumbled under her breath.

CHAPTER 2

First Day in a New Dorm

September 2, 2002

The bus pulled to the curb, and immediately Lisa boarded, with her duffel bag in one hand and suitcase in the other. She looked back and thanked God it was over. She ran to the nearest window seat to wave good-bye to all of her friends. The remaining few women stood proudly in their Class- A uniforms, ready to begin their own lives. Lisa sat back in the seat with her headphones in her ears and closed her eyes. The drive to her new school lasted barely fifteen minutes, but the anticipation made the time seem to pass more slowly. Whether she was homesick or just nervous, the mixed emotions didn't sit well in her stomach. The driver turned into what looked like a college campus. There were five buildings adjacent to each other.

"Welcome to your new home," the driver said sarcastically. One by one they exited the bus and were greeted by three airmen standing in front of what looked to be an auditorium with an eagle painted on the side. Their uniforms were impressive, neatly ironed, and starched. They wore a red rope that draped over their left shoulder and represented authority.

Lisa looked around, but there were no others in sight. The place looked abandoned.

"Where is everybody?" asked the young woman standing two feet away from Lisa. She was almost a mirror image of Lisa. Both wore their uniforms neatly starched and hair wrapped tightly, with absolutely no rank.

"Probably in there." Lisa pointed to the three-story school house across the street from them. "Why does it look like a prison?"

"Good question." She laughed. "Call me Grant, but my real name is Monique."

"Mine is Lisa, but you might as well just call me by my government name tag." She pointed to her chest.

"Fall in!" said the tallest airman standing in front of the door. He had a heavy New York accent, which was painfully noticeable. Mr. New York was handsome and muscular. His uniform fit every one of his curves perfectly. Monique's eyes traveled from his head to his boots, studying every part of what she could make out.

"Welcome to the Eagle's Nest. Come in and have a seat," the airman standing next to Mr. New York greeted them while the new airmen shoved them into the building one by one. Each student piled into a seat, waiting for further instructions.

"Not even two seconds out of basic, and I already find a man," Monique whispered to Lisa as they walked through the door.

"Which one?" Lisa eyed both gentlemen standing in the doorway.

"The one with the accent—Mr. New York." She pointed.

"I'm sure he already has a girlfriend or two." Lisa rolled her eyes.

"And I'm sure I could change that." Monique giggled to herself.

"You would probably be the first." Lisa laughed while playfully shoving Monique.

The Eagle's Nest was a giant auditorium used for meetings for all the logistics readiness students. Each day they were to report at six in the evening to discuss announcements from the training leaders.

Mr. New York walked in and screamed, "Eagle's Nest, stand by!" He paused for a minute until the female staff sergeant walked through the doors on the opposite side of the building. "Eagle's Nest, tench-hut," he continued. In unison, everyone jumped to attention. The staff sergeant stormed through the door like a bat out of hell.

"Good morning, ladies and gentlemen, welcome to your worst nightmare. You have until eighteen hundred hours to get your bags unpacked. Airman Manning here is passing out your schedule for the duration of your stay." She pointed to the other airman standing next to Mr. New York. "Your school dates are on there. Don't ask me any questions; everything you need to know is on your instructions." She paused, looking around the room as if waiting for a response, and then continued, "Your rooms will be kept clean and spotless the entire time you are here. If you fail a physical training test, room inspection, school test, or just piss me off, then you will have hell to pay. And believe me, I'm not your mother, so I don't care about you or your feelings. I show no pity for no one! Respect the rules, and we won't have a problem. You're in the military now, so I shouldn't have to hold your hand."

"Don't you just feel the love?" whispered Lisa sarcastically.

"Oh, is that what that is?" Monique whispered. "And here I thought she didn't like us."

"Fall out!" She turned to walk away, oblivious to the side conversations.

On cue, Airman Manning called everyone to attention and then dismissed the flight. They all trickled out of the building, regrouping with friends and discussing class schedules.

"My class starts next Monday with Mr. Vazquez." Monique waved her hands in the air. "I know that's right. The sooner I start class, the sooner I get out of here."

"It looks like we're stuck together for the next two months. I have Mr. Vazquez too," Lisa said, reading her class instruction.

"All right, then, where is your room? I'm on the second floor, room 235 in this building." Monique pointed to the dormitory directly across the street from the Eagle's Nest.

"Me too, but they have me on the third floor in room 301." She stuffed the paper in her right side cargo pocket. "This is some crap, and I bet they don't have elevators."

The girls grabbed their duffel bags and headed toward the building. The other dorms across from theirs were for all of the males in the squadron. As soon as they reached the glass entrance door, they were greeted by the dorm guard, who demanded to see their identification cards. Both extended the green laminated card in their neck pouches and parted ways in opposite directions.

Lisa finally made it to her room located at the end of the hall next to the emergency exit. She knocked once, hoping she was one of the ones lucky enough not to have a roommate. As soon as she walked through the door, she examined every inch of the room. There were two beds separated by a nightstand. The bed closest to the window was not occupied, so she plopped down and attempted to rest. On the other side of the room, she could see by all the pictures on the desk someone else was living there too. After a quick five-minute nap, she got up, threw her stuff in one of the nearby closets, and headed for the shower. When she finished getting ready, she headed to Monique's room.

Knock, knock.

Monique answered almost immediately. Lisa could tell she was angry about something.

"Hey, Grant, what's up?" she asked with concern. "What's wrong?"

"I come to my room to relax and take a nice hot shower, and do you know what I found?"

Lisa shrugged her shoulders.

"Hair!" Monique screamed while pointing to the bathroom. "I think I'm going to have a meeting with my roommate, because if she pulls this mess during inspection, I'm going to jail!" she shouted.

"Grant, you share that bathroom with two other women; it could've been one of them."

"Then I will have a talk with all of them," she said while adjusting her clothes in the mirror.

"Look, it's seventeen hundred. Let's go get some grub from the chow hall and then we can hit the Eagle's Nest for eighteen hundred roll call," Lisa said, pointing both fingers to the door. "Cool?" She waited for a response.

Monique rolled her eyes.

"Having an attitude is not going to make the situation better." Lisa tried to ease the tension. "Come on, we'll get some food, and when we get back we'll have a talk with all of them."

"Good, because I don't play games when it comes to my freedom, and I am not pulling extra duty over this!" Monique grabbed her hair, twisted it, and circled it into a neat bun. They were dressed in air force physical training gear, sporting tennis shoes and reflective belts with their hair tied back. They resembled each other in many ways. Both were mixed races, with matching brown hair, and were often referred to as twins.

The chow hall was located directly behind the female dormitory. As they began their journey down the road, they noticed a group of army men running and singing cadence on the opposite side.

"Hey, check those guys out," said, Lisa eyeing the soldiers. The group was organized in two perfect lines. They ran at the same speed and on the same foot. Every one of them wore black-and-gray physical training gear with matching white socks and shoes.

Neither of the two women could understand the cadence, but from what they could make out, it was not a happy ending for whoever this guy "Jody" was. Lisa took mental note of the soldier in the front with dark brown eyes and an olive complexion. The stranger was medium size, with a typical military crew cut and very little facial hair. He ran on the outside of the formation, screaming rhymes while the others repeated everything he said. She couldn't figure out if it was the man or the muscles that grabbed her attention. As he ran by, she attempted to sneak a few stares, but he already caught her looking his way. Funny thing was, she was never interested in any of the guys before, but there was something about the soldier she couldn't put her finger on.

"He looks like trouble," Monique warned, but Lisa wasn't listening. She was too busy memorizing the soldier's features.

The chow hall was packed with students waiting to sit and eat. Lisa scanned the entire room to see if she saw anyone she knew, but none of the faces looked familiar.

"Looking for me?" said a deep male voice standing behind her. She turned to see one of her good friends from basic standing directly in front of her.

"Cole!" she screamed, giving her wingman a big hug. Monique watched the reunion. "Grant, meet Cole. He was in my brother flight. Every time I found myself in trouble, he was right there to save the day." She laughed.

"She almost got into trouble over an unauthorized ruler in her portfolio, but of course, me being the Superman I am, I stuck it up my sleeve before anyone noticed." Jonathan Cole laughed, reminiscing. He was a tall, skinny fellow with a bald head. It was safe to say instead of walking around with the typical military hair cut, he decided less was always best.

"Wow, that's incredible," said Monique sarcastically as she turned her attention back to the choices on the menu.

Lisa rolled her eyes. "So where are you at?"

"We're at the security forces school up the street, but our chow hall closed, so we had to come here."

"We?" Lisa questioned, looking around.

"Oh, yeah, this is Williams," he said, pointing to the short man standing behind him with a medium build.

"Oh, okay," said Lisa, tapping Monique to get her attention. "Williams, this is my friend Grant." When Monique spun around and saw the handsome man standing in front of her, she could hardly speak.

"Hey." Monique cleared her throat. It was almost love at first sight for her, but she knew she had to play cool to avoid embarrassment. "So what brought you guys down here?"

Lisa gave her friend a puzzled look. "He just told you."

"Oh, yeah, right." Monique laughed at herself. "So, umm . . ." She scratched her head, trying to put her words into play. Williams could tell she was nervous.

"I'm Gerard or Williams, whatever you want to call me." He shook Monique's hand. "We were outside trying to make some plans for the weekend if you two aren't busy."

"Okay, Williams, did you have something in mind?" Monique gave a slight smile, still blushing from embarrassment.

"Have you heard of the BDU club?"

"What's that?" Lisa raised her eyebrow.

"Sure." Monique smiled, ignoring Lisa.

"Okay . . . if you two want to make plans, could you include us?" Jonathan interrupted. "I'm just saying."

"Huh? Oh, right. You guys game?" asked Gerard while Monique giggled.

"Sure, we'll be there." Jonathan shook his head and headed to the line.

Lisa laughed at Monique. "You've got some nerve talking about me. Where's the game face?"

"Wow, did you catch that?" Monique kicked herself for being so obvious.

"Yes, ma'am," said Lisa grabbing her tray. "What you eating?" she asked, pointing to the menu.

"Whatever won't add twenty pounds to my waistline," Monique responded.

"Then you might want to stick with the water," Lisa responded with a serious expression.

They grabbed their plates and then headed to a vacant seat. Both men followed behind while discussing plans to meet up Saturday night at the club. This was perfect for Gerard to see Monique again.

CHAPTER 3

The BDU Club

September 7, 2002

$\mathcal{S}$aturday night finally arrived, with no training leaders, training instructors, or teachers. It was time to relax and party. Unfortunately, since Monique and Lisa were new, they were still in what was called "phase one" in the new airmen program. Technical school was like living at home. As time progressed, you had to demonstrate to your training leaders, who acted as parents that you were responsible enough to wear civilian clothes and go off base. After all, you not only represented yourself but also the United States Air Force. The program was designed to help the transition process from basic military training to the military lifestyle. The higher you progressed, the more privileges you received. Phase one consisted of wearing your military uniform at all times—battle dress, service dress, or physical training gear. You were restricted from going off base or driving a privately owned vehicle, and your curfew was midnight on the weekends. For someone from the outside world, this would feel like a punishment, but to Monique and Lisa, who were fresh out of basic training, it was a new feeling of freedom. After their first week entertaining the dog and pony show for their training leaders, it was time to get loose and let their hair down. Lucky for the duo, the BDU club was only two blocks away from their

11

dormitory, so they were able to make it back before curfew. They figured they would leave around 1130 and use their training skills to run back to the dorms before roll call.

Lisa's uniform was ironed and creased to perfection. Her hair was twisted into a neat bun with a swoop to the left. There was not much a woman could do to look sexy in battle dress. The uniform did absolutely nothing to complement her figure, so trying to look cute in any kind of military uniform except for service dress was pointless. All the girls at least made an attempt to keep their eyebrows arched and nails done to show some form of a feminine side. She popped open her strawberry-flavored lip gloss and smeared on just enough to accentuate her full lips. While performing a full day of training, makeup was almost pointless. After grabbing her cap and sliding it neatly above her freshly twisted bun, both ladies were dressed and ready to go.

The club was filled with all branches of service: army, navy, marines, and air force. Lisa could not believe the amount of people packed into the tiny building. They continued through the door, mingling and rekindling with familiar faces. Music blasted from the speakers from all sides of the room. People of all ages were on the dance floor, just happy to be away from all the madness.

"This isn't that bad!" screamed Monique over the loud speakers. "Good music."

A short, stocky man quickly forced his way in the crowd to gain Lisa's attention. Her eyes widened when she noticed another one of her basic training friends, Kennedy Phillips. He embraced her with a hug while eyeing Monique through his peripheral vision.

"Kennedy? What are you doing here?" greeted Lisa.

"Partying and letting loose my stress, like everyone else in here." He smiled and then turned to Monique. "Who is this, Collier? You are holding out on me." He grabbed Monique's hand and kissed it. Kennedy was a smooth talker, but that was all he had. He was an average-looking military man with no hair and a cocky attitude. Military women were not impressed with the uniform like some civilians. If she wore one too in the same branch, the man would have to come up with another tactic to get her attention. Kennedy still hadn't grasped that concept.

"This is my friend Grant. Grant, this is Kennedy, another brother."

"Yeah, I guess you can say we're like family," he said, never taking his eyes off of her.

"Well, Collier is my sister, and I don't believe in incest." She smiled sweetly and then snatched her hand away.

Kennedy stood silently.

"Look there's Williams." Lisa pointed to Gerard.

"Ooh, how do I look?" Monique asked nervously.

"As good as you can in uniform, I guess." Lisa shrugged. "Go get your man. I'm good over here."

"All right, holler if you need me." She waved. "Bye, Kennedy."

Kennedy watched Monique sway across the dance floor to the mystery man. Gerard and Jonathan were making their way through the crowd on the opposite end. Jonathan stopped to talk to a few girls, but Gerard continued his mission to get Monique before someone else did. He slid behind her to allow traffic to pass through. Kennedy eyed his competition with envy and then sucked his teeth. "I think she's feeling me more."

"I think your uniform may be too tight and it's cutting off circulation to your brain, because Grant is not interested." Lisa rolled her eyes.

"We'll see about that," said Kennedy as he watched Monique mingle with the other man. The smile on her face indicated she shared some type of affection for him, but giving up was not an option.

"Kennedy, I'll catch you later," said Lisa, leaving him behind. She cruised around, checking out the scenery. There were a few hoots and hollers for her attention but nothing worth wasting time. She felt a presence ease behind her, so she welcomed it by dancing to the music.

"I knew I was going to find you here," said an unfamiliar voice. She turned around to see who the man could've been. It was the soldier running in formation.

"Wow, where did you come from"—she looked at his uniform—"Owen?"

"Yeah . . . Collier, I hope I didn't keep you waiting too long." He smiled.

"What makes you think I was waiting for you?"

"Well, when I caught you staring at me the other day, I figured you would try and find me."

"Sadly, you were mistaken," she said, crossing her arms.

The awkward moment of silence almost made her feel uneasy.

"Okay, I'll admit I was looking for you," he said bashfully.

"So you found me . . . mission complete." She turned to leave.

"Hold up now, we have unfinished business," he said, pulling on her arm.

"Excuse me?" she said, snatching away from his grip.

"No disrespect, little lady. I just like what I see." He eyed her from head to toe.

"And what do you want from me, sir?" She sucked her teeth.

"Your time, sweetheart, just your time." He definitely made it a point to maintain solid eye contact with her. That was always a sign of interest. Her brothers would school her on the signs of men who were genuinely interested or were just after one thing. The first sign was his eyes.

She thought about it for a moment and couldn't help but laugh. Although she would have loved to take him up on his offer, she went against her better judgment. This was a new adventure for her, and that was the first mistake most females made fresh out of basic—meet the first man who catered to her needs and then fall in love. The sad part about it was most of the females still had boyfriends at home waiting for the next phone call or love letter in the mail.

"Thanks but no thanks, Owen," she said, waving her hands. *Dear God, give me the strength to walk away from this man, please!* She was fighting every urge not to turn back and take him up on his offer. Owen was very attractive, but every man had a motive. She reminded herself she was only there for six weeks and was in no position to start something that would end up being a potential disaster. As she headed back to the center of the dance floor, she found Monique hugged up on Gerard. They had only known each other for two days, and already they were acting like a couple. Instead of disrupting the love birds, she decided to check out the other side of the club, where she found two other friends, Ashley Taylor and Anita Jefferson, sitting at one of the tables. Ashley had blonde hair and blue eyes and hailed all the way from the state of Kentucky. Anita, on the other hand, was a different story. She was born and raised on the island of Jamaica. At the age of fifteen, she moved to Miami, Florida, with her father and eventually joined the military three years later.

"What's up, ladies?" Lisa greeted, taking her seat from across the other two.

"Nothing much, just waiting on the guys to come out," said Ashley, pointing to the men's bathroom.

"Who are you talking about?" she questioned.

"You know Lloyd and Justin, right?" added Anita.

"Lloyd and Justin? Oh, yeah, Matthews and Jones. They were in the 321st Squadron, right?"

"That's right." Ashley nodded.

"Now let me find out, fresh out of prison you two already grabbed a man." Lisa laughed.

"Yes, ma'am. Apparently some chicks from the navy side tried to fight us over them. Come on now, do I look like the type of woman who should be fighting over a man?" asked Ashley, as if Lisa should have already known the answer.

"Are you serious?" Lisa shook her head.

"Sorry to break their hearts." Ashley snapped her fingers. "Well, not really."

"I'm not surprised you guys linked up." Lisa laughed. "I remember all the flirting after graduation." She thought back to when every squadron came out to the race track on graduation day to represent who were the best at PT. Each group was broken into different sets of five to six people based on who was the fastest runner. She remembered seeing Lloyd as one of the fastest in the entire wing. He could outrun anyone who challenged him.

"Yes ma'am and I too remember you and Cole did the same." Anita jumped in to support her friend.

"For your information, darling, he hasn't said more than three words to me tonight, and as you can see, I don't have a care in the world." She sat back in the chair, bobbing her head to the music.

"Don't get too comfortable, *darling*, you got a brigade of army staring your way," Ashley interrupted.

"Huh?" Lisa asked, startled. She wanted to look back but thought against it. "Hey, Taylor, can you read their names?"

"Nope. Why, what's wrong?"

"I met this guy, and now it seems I have a stalker on my hands," she said, throwing her hands up. "You give a man just a tiny bit of attention and you can't get rid of him."

"Well, I don't know how much attention you gave this guy you're speaking of, but one of them is walking over here," Ashley continued, disrupting her drama.

"Are you serious? Can he tell you're talking about him?"

"Yep, he just gave me the finger to be quiet." Ashley laughed.

"Taylor . . ."

"May I join you, Ms. Collier?" asked Owen, extending his hand for an invitation. Lisa stared at him silently.

"You know what? You two can take this table because we are going to the dance floor. Come on, Jefferson." Ashley stood up and then pulled Anita's arm.

"You can go my feet hurt are killing me," she responded, oblivious to Ashley's intention for Lisa and Owen to be alone.

Ashley poked her arm then pointed at the two. Finally Anita got the hint.

"Oh, you know now that I think about it, this is one of my favorite songs." She laughed and then exited the table. Owen sat across from Lisa, waiting for her to say something. Neither said a word. Lisa tried to avoid eye contact, so she watched the people dancing around her. She chuckled at a few who attempted to out-dance each other. Finally she focused her attention back on Owen, who'd been staring at her the entire time.

"Are you stalking me?" she broke the silence.

"No, I just don't give up on something I want."

"All these women here, why me?" She couldn't understand—out of all the beautiful women in the room, why was she the primary target?

"I like our vibe. Is that a problem?" he questioned with a raised eyebrow.

"Yes."

"Why?"

"I'm only here for a short amount of time, so I'm really not looking to get involved with anyone. Plus I don't even know you," she said sternly.

"Are you done?" He laughed.

"Yes, I am." She stood up.

"Can you please sit down? I bet if you give me a chance you would see that I'm a nice guy and not one of these sorry air force guys trying to boost your little ego."

She stood in one spot with her arms folded. Regardless of how cute or charming he was, she refused to cater to his cockiness.

"Can you please sit down?" he begged.

"Fine." She cut her eyes as she sat in her chair.

He exhaled as long as he could before continuing.

"You keep walking away from me, and you don't even realize you may be walking away from a good thing."

"First of all, your game won't work on me, so save the good thing drama. But since you choose to be annoyingly persistent, then continue . . . I'm listening." She leaned back in her chair.

"Why are you so evil?" He rubbed his hand over his neatly cut hair and then continued, "Okay, here it goes. I'm with the Fourth Signal Company at Fort Hood in Killeen, about two hours away."

"And why is a person stationed at Fort Hood down here so far away from home, and how did he and his friends get into a club intended for school folks only?"

"I'm here because I volunteered to help out with the security forces unit since they're undermanned, and one of my friends is working the door." He pointed to the entrance. "So now it's my turn. Why are you here?"

"School. How long are you here for?" The drilling continued.

"However long the air force needs me, I am here to serve. You?"

"Six weeks. There you have it. I'll be gone, and you will have to find another woman to chase and annoy."

"Are you looking for a husband or something?" He ignored the rude comment.

"No, but . . ."

"Why are you giving me a hard time about being friends? That's all I am asking. I'm sure as beautiful as you are; you get a lot of attention, so you probably think shooting down every man that approaches you is going to keep you from getting close to anyone. That's cool and all, but eventually you going to have to trust somebody."

"And who said it should be you?"

"I haven't even bought you a drink yet and you're already proposing marriage. How do you know you're even going to like me?" He laughed at how serious she was. All he wanted was a little conversation, maybe to go on a couple of dates, and she was ready to go off the deep end and get engaged.

"Not to be rude, but I haven't been in too many relationships. Since I've been here all I've seen are guys going crazy hopping from one girl to the next. So yes, I am very paranoid." She pressed her fingers against her temple and massaged the tension that was slowly forming in her head.

"Relax, Collier. If it makes you feel better, I'm not talking to anyone else. And you don't have to worry about me hopping from female to female trying to date this one and that one. I'm not that kind of guy," he reassured her.

She sucked her teeth.

"I know you don't believe me, but can I at least try and prove it to you?" He smiled as wide as he could, revealing perfectly straight teeth.

"Like I told you before, I'm not interested. Now I'm going to catch up with my friends." She pointed to the direction Anita and Ashley went. "It was nice meeting you"—she looked down at his name tape—"Owen."

"Oh, don't act like you forgot," he snapped.

She smiled again, hoping the brush off would give him a hint the conversation was over.

"Or you can call me Jerry, and don't worry, I'll see you again."

"Lisa . . . maybe next time." She winked and walked away.

"Cute . . ." His voice faded into the music.

Lisa maneuvered and found Monique, Ashley, and Anita arguing with four navy women. She rushed over, hoping to settle the dispute before it got out of hand. It was only ten thirty, and she was far from ready to go home. The crowd spread into a circle surrounding the ruthless women. Curse words and insults were flinging back and forth. Lisa knew getting in the middle of them was pointless. Gerard, Lloyd, Justin, and Jonathan were mediating so the situation wouldn't get physical. Ashley was screaming, the loudest out of the group. She was inches away from pulling hair and scratching faces. Lisa attempted to jump in between the disgruntled bunch, but the bouncer beat her to it. They were warned to end the feud or leave before security forces got involved. Lisa, Monique, Ashley, and Anita made their way to a secluded corner. Lisa watched as Jonathan chose to side with the enemy. He hugged one of the women tightly, and she returned the embrace.

"What was that all about? We haven't been here for more than two hours and already you guys are fighting?" Lisa lectured with both hands on her hips, trying to get her attention off of Jonathan.

"We didn't do anything wrong. Uncle Sam's Canoe Club is the one who decided to get mouthy with us," Monique explained with frustration in her voice.

Lisa just shook her head.

"Collier, you better get your man before the enemy does," Anita instigated.

"That isn't my man, and he is free to talk to whoever he wants to," Lisa argued.

"Forget them, I refuse to let those sea witches ruin my night," Ashley screamed to no one particular. "Now where did I put my drink?" she questioned, looking around.

"Why are you drinking? You're already fired up," Anita snapped.

"This is why we can't take you anywhere," Lisa continued.

"Hold on . . . Collier, you weren't even over here in the first place. If you would've been over here backing your friends up instead of trying to date stalkers, you would've been ready to rumble too," Ashley fired back.

"Um, maybe if you were thinking straight you would remember it was you and Jefferson that set me up in the first place to talk to him."

Ashley's eyes rolled upward, as if she were replaying a mental tape recorder in her head. "Okay, you're right. But can you believe she had the nerve to tell me Lloyd is trying to get with her? Puh-lease, that chick is U-G-L-Y," she sang.

"Okay, seriously, Taylor, you need to chill out before we get kicked out." Lisa shook her head.

"You're right about that because I'm not ready to leave," Monique hissed.

"All right, how about this since we can't take Taylor home drunk." Lisa snatched her drink away. "We need to go to the dance floor and work this steam off."

"I ain't drunk . . . I'm tipsy." She tried to stand while pointing her finger in Lisa's face but stumbled. "There's a difference."

"Right," Lisa continued, disregarding Ashley's last comment. "Let's go." She grabbed her arm, leading them to the middle of the dance floor. All four women made an attempt to enjoy what was left of the evening. When the DJ slid on a slow record, Lisa noticed Jonathan walking toward her. Her heart fluttered while her stomach flipped. She prayed her face wasn't beet red. The last thing she needed was for him to have the satisfaction of teasing her. They were like family, and she knew crossing the line would only prove to be detrimental to their friendship.

"Airman Cole reports as ordered. Would you like to dance, ma'am?" he joked.

"At ease, airman, and yes, I would love to dance." She laughed, feeling a little relieved. She wrapped both arms around his neck while he placed his arms around her waist. *Wow, thank God he can't read my thoughts.*

"So why have you been avoiding me, Ms Collier?" he asked with his lips inches away from hers.

"I haven't been avoiding you; you are the one who's been avoiding me with our rival," she joked.

"Okay, and I guess it was just my imagination seeing you all over the army guy."

"Yeah, I'm definitely not interested in that one."

She snatched away, reaching for her watch. It was already 11:00 p.m. She turned to her crew to warn them of the time. "Hey, y'all, time check."

"How about you relax? I'll let you know when you should leave." He grabbed her so they could finish dancing.

"You know we have curfew, right?"

"Look, let's just finish the song and I promise I'll let you go."
He wasn't ready to let her go. After spending the entire night
watching her with other men, he finally got his moment to dance
with her.

"If I get in trouble, Cole!" she threatened.

"It's only eleven." He glanced down at his watch. "So when
is the next time I'm going to see you again?"

"It's really up to you."

"It's up to me, huh? Well how about tomorrow at the mini
shopping center after school?"

"You mean the mini BX?" she questioned.

Jonathan nodded.

Just as Lisa was about to respond, Gerard was already
signaling to Jonathan it was time for them to leave. The 343rd
Security Forces Training Squadron was located further away from
the club then the 344th Services and 345th Logistics Squadron.
If they wanted to beat accountability, they had to leave earlier
than everyone else. He gave her a hug and asked to meet with
her later. She nodded.

She looked around, hoping to see one of her friends. After
a couple songs, she noticed Kennedy and a friend talking to
Monique. Kennedy quickly acknowledged Lisa with a hug. His
friend took notice to Lisa and began to work his charm.

"Hey, you want to dance?" He pounced over to her like a
dog in heat. "I was just telling my friend Kennedy here that when
the club is out, we should sneak back to your dorm. Where do
you stay, sweetheart?"

Lisa couldn't believe how bold these guys were. It was as if
rejection wasn't even an option. They would pick a target and
aim for the kill. Each time they missed they would reload and
aim again.

"I'm cool with the dancing part, but you coming to our dorm
is definitely out of the question, sweetheart," she mocked.

They danced a little but maintained conversation.

"So what's your name?" He licked his lips, hoping to entice
the beauty in front of him.

She looked down at her exposed name tape and gave him a confused look.

"Just what it says on my uniform." She slowly nodded, trying to be polite.

"Okay, you can call me Roberts." He ignored her.

"I'm guessing cause that's what your name tape says?"

"Kennedy tells me you're in supply. So am I," he continued, trying to put his moves into play.

She was young and innocent and knew nothing of his reputation to be a womanizer. Since she was new to the scene, that meant no one had her yet and he got first dibs. In the game of Lackland, it was all about competition, who got to whom first, and how many could you get. Lisa definitely fit the bill to be the next victim. Even though his mission was going as planned, there was slight weather change even he couldn't have predicted. Jerry had been watching the two the entire time. He wasn't ready to give up on her, and he refused to make it easy for anyone else to tempt her, especially not to some air force guy pretending to be Prince Charming. After swallowing a shot of vodka, it was time to break up the happy couple and make his final attempt. Each time she laughed at a joke or whispered in his ear, it added fuel to his fire. His dark side was a force to be reckoned with. If Roberts knew any better, he would just step away and move on to the next. At any sign of a problem, Jerry was prepared to make a solution. He stepped behind Lisa, looking directly at Roberts. When he noticed Jerry staring at him, his eyes widened, and he loosened his grip from around Lisa's waist.

"Beast? What's up man?" His voice shook a little.

"You tell me." Owens's facial expression was blank.

"Oh, I'm sorry, is this your girlfriend?" he asked, pointing to Lisa; fear was trembling from his voice. As much as Roberts loved to use and abuse his prey, fighting over them not an option.

"Something like that." Owens showed no signs of emotion, which only made Roberts more nervous.

"Beast? What kind of nickname is that?" She turned to look at Jerry. By this time, Roberts had disappeared into the crowd.

"That's something the guys call me because I'm a beast in the boxing ring." He moved his fist around, imitating a boxer.

"Okay, since when did we hook up?" She crossed her arms with a disgusted look.

"When you realized I wasn't giving up," he joked. When he noticed she wasn't laughing along, he attempted his last shot. "Come on, I'm just kidding. Besides, I know that guy. He's no good. These guys around here are nothing but pretty boys trying to play on women."

"And you aren't?" she questioned.

"Wait a minute, isn't it guys like him why you won't give me any action?" he asked, pointing toward the direction Robinson disappeared.

"Action? Owen, I was just dancing. I wasn't going to give him my number. As a matter of fact, I don't even have a phone." She stopped for a moment, crossing her arms. "Let me ask you this—since you are so stuck on getting some of my time, how would you find me anyway?"

"Just tell me where I can meet you, and I'll do it. Tell me your class schedule and I'll work around it. Where do you hang out after school? Stuff like that. I just want to see you."

"Maybe if . . ." before she could finish her sentence, Monique was running toward her, pointing to her watch. She looked down to catch a glimpse of the time, which read 11:45. "Crap, I'm late!" She shoved past him and ran out the door. The four women darted down the street, trying to beat their way home. By the time they reached the dormitory, they were all out of breath showing their identification cards to the dorm guard. Each one parted for their rooms, hoping they made it in time for accountability. Lisa's room was on the very top floor at the end of the hallway. After she nearly crawled to her door, she was out of breath and could barely speak. *I can't wait to get to second phase. To hell with this curfew . . .*

CHAPTER 4

The First Day of Tech School

September 9, 2002

School was finally here. Lisa checked herself in the mirror for any discrepancies in her uniform. She was dressed to impress in her dress blues. This was definitely a uniform where your physique mattered. The battle dress would hide your figure while the dress uniform would accentuate every curve, whether flattering or not. If a woman didn't have the body for it, her best bet was to buy a girdle and pray no one noticed. Lisa was still young with no kids, so there was no reason why she should not have been in shape. Most of the young women in the dorms were known for strutting around in their sports bras, showing off and bragging about their six-packs. After basic training, they were all fit to perfection, performing numerous pushups and sit ups on a daily basis. She adjusted her princess-cut shirt and then headed off to meet the trio down stairs.

They headed for the Eagle's Nest to form a flight and march off to school. The entire flight shined like new toy airmen. It was only 6:00 a.m., so the sun was nowhere to be found. The flight leader headed the squad to the back of the building, where the upperclassmen waited silently for the squadron commander to permit each class into the building. Lisa then spotted Roberts in the fourth group. He was secretly flirting with the girl next to him. She shook her head. Jerry was right; he was the typical tech school guy out here for fun. *What a dog.*

Class felt just like the first day of high school. Mr. Vazquez gave everyone their block one textbook. He explained each week they would receive a new binder and test. If they failed, they had one more chance. Strike two and you were recycled back a week. After eight hours of fighting sleep and taking notes, they were dismissed back to the dorms.

"Collier, I cannot stay here another week. It's bad enough I can still see basic training across the street," complained Anita.

"You won't. We'll just make sure we study together," Lisa consoled her while they walked back to their rooms.

The moment Lisa walked through the door; she dropped all of her belongings on the bed and stretched as far into the sky as she could. She examined the room to see if anything had been touched. Judging from the all of the cosmetics on the opposite desk, she figured her roommate must have made it home before her. Destiny was a sweet girl but wore way too much makeup. Lisa would wake up at 5:00 a.m. sharp and see her roommate smearing on globs of foundation. The worst part was the colors were way off of her natural skin tone. As long as she cleaned after herself and kept the room to inspection condition, Lisa could have cared less what the girl did. If she felt wearing makeup was her best way to catch a man, so be it. Destiny was in school for traffic management, which meant she was forced to endure the tech school lifestyle for a total of ten weeks. Lisa grabbed her things and locked them into her wall locker. She flew down the stairwell as fast as she could, praying silently she would catch her friends in time. They were all standing around on their cell phones and talking to other school kids. Lisa was relieved to see she wasn't left behind.

"Where are we going?" asked Lisa, a little out of breath.

"Anything but the chow hall," Ashley snapped while still holding a conversation on her cell phone.

"They got a good spot at the mini mall," answered Monique.

"Sounds good to me." Lisa smiled while the four began walking.

The mini shopping center was located between the services and security forces dormitories, a common hangout spot for all the students. It was compared to a one-stop spot; whatever you needed, they had it all. Food, fun, haircut, or essentials, the mini Base Exchange was the place to be.

A few familiar faces from the club stuck out. As they made their way inside, Lisa noticed Jerry with seven other guys she assumed were army too. She pretended she didn't see him to avoid confrontation. As she made her way to the counter to order her food, she quickly glanced his way and noticed him staring at her. The beady eyes and side conversations made her a little nervous. The group stood out among the others. They were very loud and proud about the army. Jerry and his friends were in civilian clothes and made it necessary to make their presence known to all the air force in the building. Lisa refused to give him the satisfaction of catering to their egos. If he wanted her, he was going to have to make his way to her.

"Number seven," the lady at the counter hollered.

Lisa grabbed her food and headed to the table, where the others were already sitting.

"Collier, you got an audience." Ashley had been watching Jerry watch Lisa the entire time. She couldn't understand why she was playing so hard to get. He was good looking and interested.

"I'm not interested." She tried not to smile.

"If you're not then you're stupid, because he's cute," Monique chimed in.

"In case you haven't noticed, they have been barking and showing off since we got here. I'm not sure if that's an army thing, but they can keep that over there." She laughed. "Besides, he's not even my type." She threw a fry at Monique.

"You might as well let that pride go; he's not giving up on you." Monique nodded in the direction Jerry and his friends were sitting. "And what you mean he isn't your type? You blushing, pretending not to notice him notice you, and you aren't fooling anybody but yourself. You look foolish." She threw something back toward Lisa's direction but missed.

"Whatever." Lisa rolled her eyes.

"What are you trying to prove by ignoring him?" Anita jumped in.

"Are you serious? Those guys ooze arrogance. I can only imagine how many women he has in his little black book. Now if he is serious, he'll continue his pursuit. Me, on the other hand, I'm going to make sure he understands I'm not an easy target." Lisa was rolling her neck and snapping her fingers.

"Please, he'll be under that uniform by the end of the weekend." Ashley laughed.

"Oh, really?" Lisa sucked her teeth. "Speaking of sex, I know you guys better not be giving up anything." Lisa pointed to both Anita and Ashley.

"Huh?" Anita pretended she hadn't heard the question.

"Huh hell, did you?" Lisa scolded.

"No, we just messed around . . . a little . . . maybe a little more than I wanted to, but it didn't go any further. We talked about having sex, and we both agreed now is just not the time." She took a bite of her sandwich and then put it back down.

"Taylor?" Monique interrogated.

"Maybe." She didn't take her eyes off her food.

"I hope you used some form of protection, like a condom, maybe some saran wrap?" Monique questioned, waving her hand in front of Ashley and Anita. Neither acknowledged her with as much as a glance.

"Saran wrap?" Lisa twisted her face. Monique ignored her, waiting for Ashley to answer.

"No, but we've been talking about marriage so if it happens it happens." Ashley stared back at the other three, who never took their eyes off of her. "Can we change the subject? I feel like I'm on *Cops*. And stop staring at me. I don't see you guys getting in Jefferson's face!"

"Oh, she's next," Monique reassured her.

"Look, I already told you three I didn't have sex with Justin. We just fondled, so don't try and pull me into the snake pit with Taylor." Anita glared at her friends.

"Taylor, all I know is if you are giving it up, you better be getting something out of this." Lisa laughed, throwing her hands up in defeat.

"I don't expect you guys to understand my relationship. I'm a grown woman making grown decisions, so you guys need to back off." Ashley's tone was very stern and direct. Lloyd made a promise to her that if she got pregnant he would be responsible enough to marry her. It wasn't as if he could up and disappear from her. Anyone could be tracked down in the military.

"Fine, we'll change the subject." She looked over to Lisa, who was glancing in Jerry's direction. "So, Collier, when are you going to quit this cat and mouse game and give in?"

"Now how did the interrogation turn on me? I thought we were finished with that discussion."

Before Monique could respond, Jerry was making his way in their direction.

"Ladies." He nodded to the three women who were already looking at him.

"I guess your friends are anti-social. They see four beautiful women and only one gets attention?" said Ashley with a raised eyebrow.

"It's not like that; we were wondering if these four beautiful ladies would like to join us at our table."

"Their legs broke?" asked Monique.

Jerry laughed. "No disrespect, but they didn't want to crowd you all, so they—"

"Sent a messenger?" Ashley interrupted.

"Yep." He looked over at Lisa, who was playing with her food.

They all directed their attention to Lisa, who refused to make eye contact. Ashley waited impatiently for Lisa to introduce the group. After a few minutes of silence, she took it upon herself.

"Since the cat has her tongue, I guess we'll introduce ourselves . . ." She shot Lisa an evil look. "I'm Ashley, but my last name is Taylor. This is Anita, we call her Jefferson, and Monique, but we call her Grant." She pointed at each one.

"Nice to meet you all. Is she always this difficult?" he asked Ashley.

"Funny you ask. We were just lecturing her about that," Anita interrupted.

"Okay, so I guess I'm not sitting here?" Lisa threw her fork down.

"Calm down, Collier," Monique snapped.

Jerry could see the frustration in her face and noticed she was uncomfortable. He motioned to one of his friends to call the other three over to their table, hoping to get some one-on-one time with her. When his buddy got the hint, two of them walked over to escort the ladies to their table. Lisa stayed in her seat. She could tell this was a battle she wasn't going to win.

"Look, I didn't mean for the conversation to get out of hand." He cupped his hands nervously. The plan was to pursue, not to embarrass her. Judging by her body language, she was no way in the mood for conversation.

She sat quietly for a minute and then spoke "It's all right. That's just how they are."

"We cool?" He poked his lip out.

She smiled at his efforts to make her feel better. "Yeah, we're good."

"So I'm hoping third time is a charm?"

"Third time for what?" she questioned.

"This is the third time I'm seeing you. It's obvious no matter where you go, I'm going to find you—the street, the club, now here."

"Okay, okay, I'll give you credit on the whole Prince Charming thing at the club and saving me from Roberts, and I'll even throw in an extra ten points for this 'coincidence,'" she emphasized.

"No such thing, babe—I'm it. And I'm not giving up, so you can quit with the charades and the games. I'll play any game you throw—baseball, basketball, football, whatever. It's on until you are in these arms and kissing these lips." He pointed at his muscles and then to his mouth.

"Why me?"

"Why not?"

She thought for a moment. This game was either going to get aggravating or obsessive. Either way, it wasn't going to subside. "Fine. Happy now?" She threw her hands in the air, surrendering to his demand. "Now what? You going to walk me home, hold my books, and call me late at night on the phone?" She laughed at how much she felt like they were in high school.

"Whatever you want, baby, you're my girlfriend now." He grinned. "Oh, by the way, I think it's time for you to get a cell phone."

"All right, Jerry, this is a trial period. Your mission, if you choose to accept it, is to be all that you can be," she joked.

"Isn't that the army's motto?" he quoted with pride

She grabbed her things and followed him out the door, not giving her friends a second thought. After hours of walking and talking, it was almost time for curfew. They headed back to the dormitory. She showed him her building and pointed to her window. Before she left him for the evening, she made plans to meet with him the next day, gave him a kiss on the cheek, and then entered the building. When she reached the door, she flashed her identification badge and headed for her room.

CHAPTER 5

The Middle of the Night

September 14, 2002

*K*nock, *knock.*

Lisa jumped and glanced over at Destiny, who was snoring peacefully. *I know they aren't pulling inspections this late in the night.* She looked over at her alarm clock and read 12:28.

Knock, knock.

"Coming." She stepped out of bed and walked over to the door. When she opened it, the CQ monitor was standing with an envelope in her hand. "What's up?" she said, rubbing her eyes.

"Hey, Collier, sorry to bother you, but this guy dropped this off for you." She handed her the envelope.

"What?" Lisa looked down at the envelope, but there was no name. "What guy?"

"I don't know who he was, but he paid me twenty dollars to deliver this to you. He was cute too, not a face I recognized." She grinned.

Lisa thanked her and then shut the door. When she opened the envelope, there was a necklace with a key and a folded paper. She unfolded the note and read.

Lisa,

I know it's late but I wanted you to have this. It's a key to my room. I'm staying at permanent party dorms, room 102. Don't be afraid to use it.

J. Owen

Lisa folded the letter and placed the key in her ID badge around her neck. She thought for a moment and then quickly rushed back into the bed.

"All right, Lisa, we are not going to get serious. He is just a friend," she whispered to herself.

A loud tap noise coming from the window caught her before she could drift off to sleep. *Aw man, now what?* Hoping it was just her imagination, she walked over to the window, only to see Jerry throwing rocks to get her attention. Surprised, she rushed to open it before it caught unwanted attention.

"Are you crazy?" she whispered as loud as she could.

"Come out here," he waved.

"And how do you suppose I do that?" she asked, pointing at the fact she was three stories high.

"The emergency exit next to your door."

"I can't—it will signal an alarm." She panicked.

"So? We'll be out of here before anyone notices it was you," he said, trying to convince her.

"You are crazy? *No!*" she said louder.

"Please . . ." he begged.

"If I get in trouble, we are going to fight." Lisa slammed the window shut as tightly as she could. When she turned around, she noticed Destiny was still sleeping in her bed. *Dang, she sleeps hard.* She grabbed her identification badge, slowly opened her room door, and poked her head out to see if any of the monitors were around. When the coast was clear, she slipped out and pushed the glass door open as softly as she could. In one hop, she leaped down three flights of stairs until she hit the last step. Jerry was waiting for her at the bottom, as promised.

"Now what?" She put her hands on her hips.

"Nice PJs." He tugged at her pajama bottoms.

"Focus." She laughed, pushing his hand away. "Now what?"

"Now . . ." He looked around. "We walk," he said and winked.

"Walk, where?" Lisa made a disgusted look. "You brought me out of my comfortable bed to go walking? You're crazy." She shook her hand, walking back to the dorms.

"What are you going to say to the dorm guard? Sorry I accidentally went out of the wrong exit and now I need to go back to my room?" He grabbed her arm.

She sighed.

They began to walk down the street toward the area where Jerry was staying. She prayed no one would notice the young airman walking in her pajamas. The punishment for sneaking out of the dorms with someone who was not even in school was a price she wasn't sure if she was willing to pay. Every time a car drove by them, her heart beat faster.

"You okay?" Jerry asked, noticing Lisa constantly looking over her shoulders.

"How much farther?" She scanned the area, looking to see if anyone noticed her.

"Right there." Jerry pointed to the permanent party hotel located a block away from the mini BX.

"So you thought you could get me out my room for what?" she asked.

"Just wanted some privacy away from all the distractions." They walked toward a room facing the parking lot on the first floor. He unlocked the door, pushing it open just enough for her to slip through.

"Yeah right," she muttered.

When she entered the room, she noticed it was a lot cleaner than she expected for a man. She studied his pictures displayed on his nightstand, clothes hung neatly in the open closet, and the equipment he had set up: PlayStations, stereo, speakers. He watched her walk to each area of the room, picking the items up one by one and then putting them back.

"Would you like to sit here with me?" He patted the empty space on the bed next to where he was sitting.

"Sure." She smiled, placing his PlayStation controller back on the dresser she'd been playing with.

When she sat next to him, he shifted closer to her. He lifted her chin to him and looked into her eyes.

"Anybody ever tell you, you have very pretty eyes?" he smiled.

"No, but—"

Before she could finish, he gently kissed her bottom lip.

Startled, she jumped back. "Um, no but—"

He interrupted her again with a full kiss on her lips. She grabbed his hand off her face and placed it back on his lap. In one swift motion, he pulled her down, cradling her like a newborn, and kissed her. This time she surrendered.

"You are so beautiful," he said and stared.

Lisa couldn't believe how easy she gave in, but every moment was well worth it. He smiled at her innocence and sweetly whispered, "I'm glad you're mine now." Her heart and mind were racing. *What did I just do?*

CHAPTER 6

The Final Phase

September 27, 2002

After four weeks, Lisa finally reached phase three. This phase meant she had no curfew on the weekends and she was able to go off base wearing only a bra and underwear if that's what she felt for the day. Since the first night Lisa and Jerry spent together, they were almost inseparable. Jerry showered her with notes, flowers, and dinners. Now that she was in the final phase, they could go on a real date downtown, as opposed to hanging around base.

It was another day in class for Lisa but almost close to the end. They finally reached block five, with only one and a half weeks away from graduation. Lisa sat quietly in class waiting for three o'clock to hit. Once they were dismissed, she planned to meet up with Jerry. Then they would barricade themselves into his hotel room for the entire weekend until it was time for Sunday night accountability. She stared at the clock intensely, as if she could magically make the hands move. Each time the seconds hit, she would tap her pen on the desk. The last hour was taking too long to pass, which only made Lisa more anxious.

"You are really out of it today, I take it we have another date with Private First Class Owen?" whispered Monique, breaking Lisa out of deep thought.

"Huh?" Lisa jumped. "Oh, yeah." She sighed while watching her teacher lecture to the entire class. "Shouldn't Mr. Vazquez be teaching the assignment and not his life story?" Lisa rolled her eyes the grey-haired, chubby man standing in front of the classroom not paying the two any attention.

Mr. Vazquez was retired air force and bragged about his job as if it were the best in the entire military. You would have thought logistics was a special task force or something. The stories he would tell seemed a bit exaggerated, but the students had no choice but to entertain them. Others in the class even acknowledged him with a question or two to learn more about what life was like outside the real air force.

"Did I mention he's boring?" Lisa growled.

"You're preaching to the choir. I'm the one that got my 341 pulled for falling sleep." Monique chuckled. The 341 was a small air force form that was carried by an air force trainee at all times. If the airman was caught doing something wrong, anyone who held the title of sergeant or higher could take it and report them to their training leader. It could also be pulled for something positive, but at Lackland Air Force Base, that rarely happened.

"Forget him. He's so stuck on himself. We only have eight hours of class time and he spends seven hours and thirty minutes talking about his life. I doubt he even turned them in to the training leaders," said Lisa, staring around the room, watching her classmates bob their heads, attempting not to fall asleep. She turned her attention to Ashley, who was already in a coma-like state. "Hey, look at Taylor. She's about to bust her head on the table." Lisa nudged Monique's arm. "Get her before Mr. Vazquez takes her 341."

"Taylor!" whispered Monique. Ashley didn't budge. "She won't wake up." She turned back to Lisa.

Lisa looked around the room for Mr. Vazquez, who was too busy reminiscing back to his days in basic training. When the coast was clear, she threw her pen and hit Ashley in the head. Ashley jumped, knocking her book to the floor. Monique and Lisa secretly chuckled.

"Let me tell you, ladies. It was funny. Even to this day if it wasn't for my uniform being so clean and crisp, that drill sergeant would've noticed we wrecked his car." He laughed hysterically before continuing on with the lesson plan. Both women looked at each other confused.

"What is he talking about?" Lisa whispered to Monique.

"I just don't know." Monique shook her head.

"All right now, we just got in phase three. Any mess up it's back to one, and I refuse to keep having these curfews like I'm back at my mommy's house. I work way too hard, and this weekend it's about me and Jerry." Lisa slapped her best friend a high five.

"Yeah, I think I'm going to see what Gerard is up to."

"I'm guessing things are going well between you two."

"I guess you can say that. I think he's cute and all, but you know Kennedy thinks he's bad news. He told me Williams has a few women back in security forces." Monique thought for a moment and then continued, "It's whatever, I'm not looking to get married. I'm just trying to have fun." She cleared her throat. "Um . . . by the way, Cole has been asking about you."

Lisa was thrown completely off guard. The sound of his name gave her butterflies. As much as she would have loved to pursue a relationship with him, she couldn't cross that line. In basic he was an element leader in her brother flight, just like she was. The element leaders marched in the front of the flight in every formation. This was good for Lisa because that was exactly how she met her knight in dirty camouflage. They would secretly whisper to each other, having detailed conversations when the training instructors weren't looking. This connection helped develop a deep brother-and-sister bond. Since then they would give each other hugs and speak when passing through, but it never went deeper than that, mainly because they both were afraid to take it further.

"Okay and you're telling me this because . . ." She waited impatiently.

"Don't get on the defense with me. I'm just letting you know you've been neglecting your BFF responsibilities," she joked.

"No, I haven't. I've been catering to your needs and wants ever since the first day I laid my eyes on this beautiful face." She grabbed Monique's cheeks playfully.

"Aw, that's really sentimental and everything, but I think it's time you take some time out of your busy schedule and maybe hang out with him. Just let him know that there is still a friendship there."

"Why is this so important to you?"

"Because I think it will be fun for us to double date," Monique snapped.

"Okay, okay I'll pencil him in." Lisa looked to Monique for approval. Monique smiled to say she was pleased. "I'm not going to sleep with him, so don't ask." She was pointing her finger in Monique's face with a serious expression.

"I could care less if you two played miniature golf. All I'm asking is you to do is spend some quality time with your basic training brother." She paused to sip her soda that was sitting on the table. "Besides, isn't that what y'all are telling everybody you two are? This is my brother, this is my sister," she imitated Lisa in a childlike voice.

"You are so fired." Lisa couldn't help but to laugh at her best friend's impression of her.

As soon as the class was dismissed, the flight marched back to their dorms in preparation for the weekend. After spending a reasonable amount of time showering and preparing for the evening, she headed off to meet her soldier. She tiptoed her way through Eagle's Lodge so no one would get suspicious. When she finally made it to the door, she stuck her key in the lock and turned the knob. The room was empty, and there was no sign Jerry ever made it off of work. He worked the morning shift and was normally off before three. She looked around the room to see if he left a note or some sign he would be returning. *Maybe he's still at work.* She maneuvered around the room, looking through his closet and drawers. When she made her way back to the nightstand, she opened it to find stacks of paper crumbled on top of each other. She grabbed a few scraps of paper with phone numbers scribbled on them.

"Housekeeping," said the maid as she pushed open the door.

Lisa gasped and then dropped all of the paper on the floor.

"Oh, sorry, ma'am, I'll come back later." She smiled at Lisa as she closed the door behind her.

"That's what I get for being nosy," Lisa mumbled to herself. Her heart was still racing. She picked everything up and placed it neatly back into the nightstand.

After three hours, Jerry still hadn't shown up. She called his cell phone three times but was sent to voice mail. This wasn't like Jerry to disappear or turn off his cell phone.

"Jerry, I refuse to wait all night for you. I'm headed back to my room," she yelled into the receiver and then hung up the phone. Disappointed, she quickly grabbed her belongings and headed back to her dorms, hoping the night wasn't completely ruined. The plan was to relax for the evening, but unfortunately Jerry seemed to have other plans, which didn't include her.

It was a perfect September evening, the kind when a couple could go on a real date and just enjoy each other in peace. She inhaled the fresh air as she watched the sun slowly disappear. Toward the end of the night, she could always hear the trainees in basic across the long field screaming at the top of their lungs. Most of them were sounding off to either the air force song or just some random nonsense to their training instructor before heading off to prepare for the next day. Every day before accountability, she would sit outside and listen to them. The dormitory was packed with people everywhere. She roamed through the campus until she reached her dorm. The dorm guard was hovering over a fellow classmate who was obviously not the slightest bit interested in what she had to say. Lisa flashed her ID and proceeded through the door. The guard barely gave her a second look. Women maneuvered in and out of the small hallways in roller sets and bath robes. Most of them were either on their cell phones or making their way to the day room for TV time. The night was too young to go to sleep, so she headed up the steps to check on her fellow comrades.

Monique was getting ready for the club with Ashley and Anita when Lisa knocked on the door and interrupted what sounded like a private all-girl party.

"Ladies," said Anita, opening the door wider for the other two to see who was at the door. "Our threesome just became a foursome."

"What happened with Jerry?" Monique asked, puzzled.

"He wasn't there, so I decided to come out with my girlfriends. What's on the agenda for the evening?" asked Lisa, plopping down on Monique's bed.

"BDU club, of course, but this time we're going out like women," said Anita, implying the uniform made women in the military look like men.

"I guess I'll tag along. I have nothing else to do," agreed Lisa since she refused to stay in for the evening. She climbed off the bed to check herself in the mirror. Even though she didn't have anyone to impress, stepping out the door with her friends looking less than perfect was an absolute no go. She untied her neat, smooth ponytail and began to flatten her hair. Satisfied at the reflection, she reached for the lotion on the desk and smeared it across her legs. The other girls were applying the finishing touches to their outfits, and all headed out the door.

People covered every inch of the streets, crowding the entrance to the club. There was no sign of order, just anxious students ready to have a good time.

"What's going on tonight?" questioned Anita, passing by a group of guys who were trying desperately to get her attention.

"No, the real question is, who are all these people? They can't all be students. This base ain't but so big." Ashley was looking around at the crowd.

"Hey, there's Williams!" Lisa pointed toward the door, tugging Monique for her attention. He recognized Monique and signaled for her to come to the front. While bypassing the crowd, a stranger grabbed Lisa's arm before she made it to the dorm.

"What?" she said with an attitude at the tall, medium-build man with the New York baseball cap hovered over his eyes.

"Hello Miss." He lifted his cap a little so she could get a better look at his face. "You don't recognize me, do you?" He waited for her response.

"I'm sorry, am I supposed to?" She folded her arms, looking the stranger up and down.

"When you got here, I greeted you at the door with a cute face and a nice smile." He smirked.

"Oh, yeah, Mr. New York, okay. I'm sorry, I didn't recognize you in civilian clothes." She pointed to his attire.

"Mr. New York?" he questioned. "Is that supposed to be some kind of nickname?"

"What am I supposed to call you?" She placed both hands on her hips.

"Perez or Emmanuel," His eyes were roaming up and down her legs, trying to get a quick glimpse of her package before she caught him. Judging by the grin on his face, he was impressed by the beauty in front of him. "It must be nice to be able to avoid this long line"

"Oh, that's why you grabbed me, so I can take you to the front?" she asked playfully.

"No, nothing like that. I just wanted to say hi."

"Hi, may I go now?" She laughed, pointing to the door.

"Yes, ma'am. Save me a dance." He winked.

It's amazing how sweet and friendly men are when their hormones are raging. She laughed at the idea of entertaining Emmanuel. Jerry would have a fit. Even though they weren't exactly committed, Jerry was very strict about respect. The worst thing anyone could ever do was disrespect him, especially since he'd been so good to her these past couple of weeks, buying her "I'm thinking of you" gifts, writing her cute little notes, or enjoying their quiet walks around the base getting to know each other. He may not be permanent, but he was a keeper for now. She managed to shove through the line to get back to her friends, who were waiting for the bouncer to finally let them in. Lisa recognized he was one of Jerry's friends. When the familiar face noticed hers, he smiled and then allowed them to pass. The moment they entered the club, there was wall-to-wall people. None of the girls had enough breathing room, let alone space to walk around. Anita shoved her way to a nearby empty booth and climbed in. It was perfect for the evening. They could see any and everyone who walked in. Lisa watched the door, hoping to see Jerry. Maybe when he got home and noticed she wasn't there he would figure she was at the club and just come on down. After an hour of watching, there was still no Jerry, and the club was only getting more crowded.

"I want to dance, forget this!" Anita stood up on the seat and began grinding to the music.

"Hell, why not? Can't dance anywhere else!" Monique stood up to dance next to her.

Lisa and Ashley stayed in their seats, watching people pour in through the entrance.

"They need to call the fire marshal; they have to be breaking some kind of law!" Ashley screamed over the loudspeaker that was located to her left.

Lisa nodded in agreement. All she wanted to do was be at the hotel with Jerry and watch movies, and here she was at this club with a bunch of unknown faces. She noticed Cole moving throughout the crowd. She tried to get a better look, but the enormous amount of people blocked her view. After a couple of minutes passed, she noticed him again, this time he was with what looked to be one of the navy girls Ashley was squabbling with a couple weeks prior.

"Hey, Grant, it looks like my BFF isn't thinking about me at all. He's too busy dancing with the enemy," Lisa said with much attitude intended.

"Huh?" Monique looked into the crowd, where she noticed Cole with the same navy women from the other night.

"Forget him." Ashley sucked her teeth.

"I plan to," Lisa responded quickly.

Anita and Monique continued dancing as if no one was watching. Monique stepped onto the table and continued shaking her hips. Lisa shook her head and laughed at her friends' behavior. Monique was far from shy, and she loved the attention. Emmanuel and his company made their way to Lisa's table, where they could see the two beautiful women dancing carelessly on top of the table. One of the guys pulled Monique off to dance with him. In a few seconds, she vanished into the crowd without a trace. Anita jumped off the seat and began dancing in the middle of the crowd. Emmanuel slid into the booth, looking at Lisa and Ashley.

"Hey, New York," said Lisa.

"What's up, country?" he shot back.

"Excuse me? I'm not country, I'm Southern, and there is a difference," she snapped.

"Okay, Southern, would you like to dance?"

Lisa looked around the room to see wall-to-wall people and no space. "Where?"

"Come with me." He grabbed her arm and slid out of the booth. "I'll make room for you." He continued while she followed him to the middle of the dance floor. After a few minutes of dancing, Lisa began to feel smothered by all the people surrounding her. She tried to push a couple of the guys in front of her to move forward, but they were only getting more out of control. By this point, even Emmanuel was annoyed by the rowdy men in front of them. He swung Lisa around, tapped one of the men on the shoulder, and signaled for them to move. When each one turned around, she recognized them as friends of Jerry. She quickly jumped in front of Emmanuel before words could be exchanged.

"Smith!" She smiled at the angry bull blowing steam from his nostrils. Smith was six foot five, with broad shoulders and a mustache. To a stranger off of the street, he was quite intimidating, but to his friends, he was a pretty nice guy. "You want to be careful? You just bumped into me," she said playfully.

"Where's Owen?" he questioned, staring at Emmanuel.

"I waited, but he never showed up. He didn't leave a note or anything. So I came out with my friends. I was kind of hoping you could tell me where he's at."

Smith and Emmanuel were inches from touching head to head, and neither bothered to acknowledge her.

"Hey . . . Smith, what's going on?" Her eyes shifted back and forth to both men, who deeply engaged in a stare down. "Hey, Perez, do you know Smith? He's friends with my boyfriend." Neither of the two said a word.

Lisa's hair stood on end. She knew something bad was about to happen. *Is he really going to fight with Perez because we were dancing?* Her mind was racing; it wasn't like she was doing anything wrong, but the look in Smith's eyes and noticing the four other men standing behind said differently. She could see Emmanuel wasn't backing down, nor was he afraid of the five soldiers standing in front of him.

"Do we have a problem here?" Smith spoke with a deep Texas accent. He was originally born and raised in the hardcore streets of Dallas. On a good day, Smith was the clown out of the bunch, but tonight he and his friends were dressed in black from head to toe, ready for war.

Emmanuel laughed at Smith's threatening tone. "If you know what's best for you, I'd suggest you get out my face." He looked around at the men in front of him, "Oh, I forgot, I guess you're the tough guy now you have your toy soldiers with you." He began walking closer to Smith. "Look here, I'm not fighting over a female, but if you think I'm afraid, you better think again. You may not realize this, but you are a bit outnumbered in here, so it wouldn't be your smartest move, my man." He motioned around to the gentlemen standing behind him.

Lisa couldn't believe the scene that was unfolding before her very own eyes. The army guys gathered around Smith; the air force guys were not too far behind Emmanuel.

"So I guess it's going to be the army versus the air force tonight," Emmanuel said with a smirk on his face. He reached under his shirt to expose his P99 semi-automatic pistol. In one quick moment, Smith swung his fist and landed directly onto Emmanuel's jaw. Blood spurted from his mouth, and he fell to the floor. Before he could react, three army men jumped on top of him and began kicking him to the ground. Lisa froze at the bloody sight. Two air force members attempted to grab Smith, but he was able to shake each one off like rag dolls. Three more air force members came out of nowhere and pulled the soldiers off of Emmanuel. His lip was bleeding and his shirt was torn, but he was still swinging for anybody he could hit.

He pulled out his weapon and charged for Smith, and both men fell to the floor. Smith tried to grab the weapon but knocked it out of Emmanuel's hand. Lisa's feet were paralyzed to the floor. Ashley ran behind her, pulling her away before she was hit. From the corner of her eye, she saw Jerry running in to help Smith. He pulled Smith to his feet and then pushed Emmanuel to the ground and kicked him one good time. Jerry picked up the pistol and began hitting Emmanuel in the face with the butt of the gun. He slid the weapon into his pants and headed toward the direction of where Lisa was standing. As he began walking towards her, security forces was already on their way inside the club. Six cops and two K-9s stood at the door, each one with a 9-millimeter ready to go hand in hand with anyone who wouldn't follow protocol. The crowd dispersed within seconds. The soldiers regrouped and headed out the back door while the air force guys escaped through the front, dragging Emmanuel's limp body.

Lisa ran out of the club as fast as she could. Her heart was beating a thousand times a minute, while her mind raced. The idea of Jerry fighting made her sick to her stomach. When she finally made it to her building, she grabbed her chest and sank to the ground. Out of breath and barely able to move, she didn't notice Jerry sneaking up behind her.

"Hey." His facial expression was blank.

"Hey," Lisa jumped. "What was that about?" She asked out of breath still holding her chest.

"I should be asking you the same thing, seeing as though when I'm not around you can do whatever you want. It's funny how this whole time I've been trying to prove to you that I'm a good man and I don't want to hurt you or use you. But it never dawned on me that the one that should've been worried was me."

"Jerry, are you crazy? You and your friends could have been killed in there," she asked, gasping for air.

"I thought you were coming to my room tonight." He ignored her. "I walked in and Lisa was nowhere to be found." He grabbed his head and then turned back to her direction. "I knew you were at the club, and I watched you all over him for quite a few songs. That's why he got what he deserved. As for us, we are through." Jerry walked closer to her. She backed away, fearing what he may do to her. He felt around her chest and then yanked the key that dangled around her neck. "You won't be needing this."

She couldn't put the pieces together. *What just happened?* He was breaking up with her because she was dancing with someone else. Two men fought because they were in different branches. The whole night was unbelievable.

"Jerry, you are breaking up with me because I was dancing with someone else? This is crazy."

"No, I'm ending this because trusting you was a mistake. It's not about dancing with other men, it's about respect—respect you can't seem to show me."

"Jerry, you're crazy. This scene, here, it's crazy!" She stood to her feet. Lisa could feel the tears in her eyes but refused to let them show. Her eyes focused to the ground before she continued. "So just like that, it's over?"

He didn't answer.

CHAPTER 7

Another Day in Class

September 30, 2002

"*I* knew I was a fool." Lisa shook her head, trying to avoid Mr. Vazquez's lecture on women and their place in the military.

"No, you weren't. You got involved with the infamous tech school fling and came to realize Jerry was crazy." Monique was copying the notes from Lisa's paper.

"I feel like Jerry was only using this as an excuse to dump me. He was probably seeing some another woman anyway."

"Why did Perez start that fight anyway?" Monique questioned.

"Don't get me started on Perez. What is this whole air force versus army feud? He had the nerve to disrespect me. Can you believe that?" Lisa slammed her hand on her notebook.

"What you expect? These guys are hardcore hoodlums, wearing a uniform and portraying themselves to be these patriotic veterans fighting for freedom. That's a no-go." Monique rolled her eyes.

"Break time, be back in twenty minutes," interrupted Mr. Vazquez to his class, who was already half sleep.

Monique and Lisa stood up, heading for the door. They quietly walked down the right side of the hall to avoid any training leaders or teachers screaming at them. Once the coast was clear, they sped into the snack room. Ashley was hunched over in the corner, trying to fix her uniform pants.

"Taylor, you okay?" Lisa kneeled beside her.

"No! These stupid shirt suspenders broke off while I was marching and popped me in the leg" She rubbed her leg. "When is lunch? I'm hungry!" she asked irritated.

"In about forty-five minutes." Monique was looking down at her watch.

"Jefferson told me about the fight between you and Jerry," Ashley stood to her feet adjusting her shirt in the mirror next to the refrigerator.

"It was so dramatic. He chased me to the dorm, snatched his room key from around my neck, and broke up with me." Lisa shook her head as hard as she could make sense of the evening.

"Come on now." Ashley rolled her eyes. "Yes, it was a very dramatic night, and he had every right in the world to be upset with you. You know that."

"Whatever, Taylor, it was stupid and dangerous. Jerry overreacted, period," Monique cut in before Lisa could respond.

"Whatever. You say you want a good man but will push him away for anything." She stood up, shaking her head at Lisa, who was still kneeling down. "You seen him get into one fight, and all of a sudden this man is so dangerous. So he's a little temperamental. At least you know he cares about you. He was fighting because he felt disrespected. Put yourself in his shoes. Imagine walking in a club to find him all over another woman." Ashley sighed.

"I understand that, but he ended it with me, not the other way around," she defended.

"Stop and think about his feelings and where he is coming from. Instead of making yourself the victim, why don't you put yourself in his shoes?" Lisa slumped over, replaying thoughts of the evening in her head.

"It will be okay." Ashley embraced her with a hug before returning to class.

Lunchtime was finally here, and as usual, the girls were in the front of the line ready to get their food.

"My stomach is touching my back!" shouted Ashley.

"Why have you been eating so much?" Monique questioned.

"I have a high metabolism." She said proudly.

"You're probably pregnant," spat Anita.

"That better not be it, Taylor," Lisa jumped in.

"Calm down, Mom. It wouldn't matter because we've been talking about marriage."

"And so just like that, wedding bells and baby carriages. Let me guess, you already got our ugly bridesmaids dresses picked out," Monique joked.

"What you think?" She lifted her hand to show off her gold promise ring on her finger.

"Gee, it's been what three weeks?" Lisa asked sarcastically.

"For your information, it's been eleven weeks. I met him before we boarded the plane for basic training." She giggled playfully.

"Oh, my goodness." Monique couldn't believe her ears. "So tell me this, Bridezilla, where is he getting stationed?"

"We find out next week." She grinned.

"Let me get this straight, you are trying to marry a man you've known for a little over two months and you don't know where he's getting stationed?" Monique lectured.

"First off, Grant, since you want to be judgmental with me, when are you going to worry about your own man and stay out of our lives?" Taylor snapped.

"Whenever I do, it won't be eleven weeks from now," Monique responded.

"All right, you two," Anita interrupted.

They entered the chow hall, getting their food and sitting at their favorite table. Just then Jonathan, Kennedy, and three of their friends walked in.

"Hey, Kennedy," shouted Monique.

"Could you two be any louder?" Ashley yelled.

Monique ignored her when the crew approached the table. Out of nowhere, Jonathan jumped on Lisa, embracing her with a big hug.

"Good afternoon!" he screamed.

"Get off me!" She playfully pushed him off of her.

"Please take that somewhere else," snapped Anita

"My apologies, ladies," he greeted while adjusting his uniform and then turned his attention back to Lisa. "Where have you been? What's up with that Owen guy? You mad at me?" he interrogated her.

"Let me try to answer you accordingly." She laughed "I've been here, he is out of the picture, and no, I'm not mad at you."

"Aw, really?" He smiled.

"I don't need your lecture. It's bad enough I left one mommy in Maryland to come here and have three." She pointed to her entourage.

"We love you too." Monique was offended and then turned her attention to Kennedy. "So what are y'all up to?"

"Our chow hall is closed again, plus when I saw the most beautiful girl in the squadron, you know I had to drop in and say hello." He grinned from ear to ear. Monique slightly smiled at his efforts to flirt.

He attempted to move his chair closer to hers as she moved in the opposite direction.

"Um, Kennedy, can you move over just a little? I kind of like my space." Monique gestured.

"In other words, she's not interested, so move your little behind over to the next table," Ashley motioned.

Kennedy was clearly embarrassed. Ashley never cared for him too much, considering he gossiped more than your average female. While the group continued their conversation, Jonathan noticed Gerard and headed toward his direction. Lisa waved and signaled for him to come over, but he brushed off her invitation by turning the other way.

"What's up with him?" questioned Lisa.

"We broke up," Monique answered.

"He's mad because I pulled all his cards on the table and told Grant the truth about his little dormitory rendezvous. Both of them are out here chasing after other women and they have the nerve to come and try to talk to people I care about. That's not going to happen while I'm around," Kennedy interrupted.

Lisa glared at Monique, but she didn't respond. Monique was never one to believe everything she heard, but just a tiny shed of doubt could easily push her away. She refused to let Gerard break her heart. The hurt in his eyes was enough to cut her like a knife. She wanted to ask him why would he lie and play with her affection. They spent many secret nights away in abandoned buildings getting to know each other away from the crowd. Neither one of them had a car, so maneuvering far from the campus was a difficult task. The bus only stopped in certain areas of the base. Kennedy was proud to show he was the victorious one, even if it meant lying to win over the woman he wanted.

CHAPTER 8

Final Week of School

October 11, 2002

The weekend lockdown was finally over. After an investigation, the training leaders were unable to pin the fight on anyone, so they decided to free all of the students from their prison cells. Lisa and Monique walked to the mini BX for ice cream to celebrate their freedom. People crowded the entire area, breathing in the beautiful Texas air. Lisa noticed Gerard again, but this time his expression showed no sign of friendship. He brushed past the two, nearly knocking Lisa out of the way. He stared in Monique's direction as she returned the glare. Neither of the two said a word. Monique continued walking, trying not to make a scene in front of the large crowd standing around the store.

"So just like that, it's over?" Gerard asked through clinched teeth.

"We talked about this. There is no reason to bring this back up," Monique whispered.

"You're making a big mistake," he said, brushing past her to walk away. Monique watched him walk away.

"What was that about?" Lisa asked frustratingly.

"He called me a few times and I sent his calls to voicemail. I refuse to let that man make a fool out of me." She said sternly.

"Are you sure about this?" Lisa stood in front of Monique with her arms folded.

"I know what I'm doing." Monique's expression was blank.

"I don't think you do." Monique ignored her and continued to walk. Lisa jumped in front of her, blocking the entrance to the store. "You know I love you, but you're making a big mistake leaving him. He makes you really happy, and he's a good friend."

"Why do you care?" Monique crossed her arms.

"Because I love you, and so does he," Lisa continued. "Please, just try."

Monique watched him as he was walking away. The idea of never seeing him again stung deep into her soul. She shook her head and then focused her attention on Lisa. Unlike the other couples, Monique and Gerard were very private about their affairs. This not only avoided drama but also kept unnecessary negativity out of the relationship. Gerard was the best boyfriend she'd ever had in her short life. Deep down, she knew Lisa was right.

"You make me sick." Monique sucked her teeth.

Lisa smiled. "That's because you know I'm right."

October 21, 2002

Graduation wasn't too far away. The final block was here. After six weeks of stress, Lisa finally made it to block seven.

"With a 97 percent average, honor graduate has been awarded to Airman First Class Ashley Taylor." Mr. Vazquez handed Taylor her plaque. The class applauded while she shook his hand then headed for her seat.

"You go girl," said Lisa, giving her friend a hug.

"I can't believe I'm actually saying this, but congratulations." Monique smiled.

"Thank you." Ashley embraced Monique.

"So I take it we are all celebrating graduation tonight?" Monique suggested.

"Can't, Lloyd graduates today, and I'm going to celebrate with him." She looked down at her watch. "As of right now, he should be getting ready to get his plane ticket. I think we are going to get a hotel for the evening," Ashley continued.

"Okay, what about you?" Monique turned to Lisa.

"I'm all yours for the night," said Lisa with a grin on her face.

"Sounds good. You putting out?" Monique winked.

"Only if you're paying." Lisa laughed.

"I'm guessing you and Jerry still haven't patched things up?" she questioned Lisa.

"No, ma'am. As a matter of fact he made it perfectly clear on my voice mail to lose his number, either that or give it to my new boyfriend Perez if he wants a round two." Lisa giggled at the immaturity.

"Whoa." Monique's eyes widened.

"I'm okay. After a couple of nights of crying, I was back to my normal state of mind. What about you and Williams?"

"I made up with him." Monique thought long and hard to the night she crept into the security forces dormitory, hoping no one could spot she was an outsider. After several attempts to locate his room, she gave up. Lucky for her, Gerard was on his way home from the club when he spotted her leaving the dorms. She quickly gave him a hug and begged him to forgive her. Monique was never the one to be so dramatic, but desperate times called for desperate measures. His duty station was clear across the United States at Nellis Air Force Base in Nevada. Both knew the long distance would be a challenge.

"Well, I'm glad at least one of us is happy," Lisa interrupted Monique's train of thought.

Both women giggled.

"Seriously, we need to figure something to do since this is the last time we're going to get to hang out for a long time." Monique frowned.

"Well, club's out. We can party in the parking lot," Lisa suggested.

"Sounds fun to me, Grandma, let me know what time."

"Cool."

The girls packed their things to get ready to be dismissed. After showering and changing their clothes, all four girls headed to the mini BX. Lisa was the first to enter the building when she saw Lloyd hugging on another woman. The shock paralyzed her from the waist down.

"Oh, no," Lisa blurted out. Ashley brushed past her, frozen at the sight of the couple.

"What the . . ." she snapped. Lloyd jumped in front of the woman, blocking her view of Ashley.

"Lloyd, what's going on?" the unknown woman questioned.

"Yeah, *Lloyd,* what is going on?" Ashley's eyes were tearing up.

Lloyd stood silent for a moment. He knew the truth would hurt the woman he'd grown to care for deeply. "Ashley, this is my wife." He wanted to apologize, but pride wouldn't allow him to admit his guilt.

Stunned, Ashley's eyes shifted from Lloyd to the woman who was obviously clueless to what was going on. She grabbed her pregnant stomach.

"Are you really going to stand there and act like you and Taylor were not a couple this whole time?" hollered Monique so that everyone around could hear.

"Look I wanted to tell you but . . ." he tried to explain.

"But what? I guess all the times we slept together you neglected to mention you had a wife!" Her voice grew louder.

"Tanya . . ." He turned back to his wife, whose face was hard and expressionless. Ashley's words replayed in her mind.

"Don't even Tanya me. All this time I've been home supporting you, paying your bills, sending you letters, and you're cheating on me!" she threw her hands in the air.

"Oh, Tanya, did he also neglect to tell you I'm five weeks pregnant with his child?" said Ashley.

Tanya covered her mouth, shaking her head. Her eyes were swollen.

"Yes, we started messing around when we stayed at the hotel the day before we left for basic training, but that was only the beginning." Ashley continued, "Oh, yeah, and this cheap ring on my finger was his promise we would be getting married, but that's not going to happen seeing as though you're already committed." She waved it in front of Tanya. Lloyd's jaw tightened.

"She's lying. I never slept with her." Lloyd grabbed Tanya's arms, trying to take her attention off of Ashley and back to him. "Come on, we been together for six years. Why would I mess that up for this?"

"Is that why I couldn't come see you when you left for training? Because of her?" Tanya was stunned.

"He didn't want you to come because we got a hotel for the day and that was the first time we made love!" Ashley screamed.

"Ashley, you and your imagination is getting way out of hand. You might want to leave before you say something you are going to regret," he said through clenched teeth.

Ashley's tear-filled eyes couldn't believe the man she loved could be so heartless to her. She watched him as he tried to comfort his outraged wife.

"Tanya, don't believe her—she's crazy!" Lloyd continued to plead his case. "First of all, Ashley, I told you I didn't want you. I told you I was married, and now you got your friends lying for you?" Lloyd lied.

"Lloyd, is she lying or are you lying?" Tanya glared at Ashley.

"She is!" He spat, staring at Ashley.

"I've had enough!" Monique screamed while charging toward Lloyd. Lisa quickly jumped in between.

Lloyd grabbed his wife's hand and proceeded to walk in the opposite direction. Ashley watched as he walked away and began to chase after him.

"I'm going to get you for all you got when this baby comes! Watch, I'm taking you for everything you got! How dare you treat me this way?" Ashley was yelling at the top of her lungs while Anita was holding her down, trying to keep her from making any physical contact with him.

"Come on, let's get her out of here" Monique quickly grabbed Ashley out of Anita's arms and pulled her towards the exit door, the others followed while the crowd watched.

Deep down Lisa knew this was going to happen. Ashley knew nothing about him. This kind of scene wasn't new in tech school; it was way too common for someone to have found their "soul mate," just to find out it was merely wishful thinking. She watched her friend cry, only to imagine this being her a few weeks from now. After all, she didn't know much about Jerry either, and already they'd had sex without protection. She held her stomach. *I think I need a test.*

All four women sat in the Eagle's Nest waiting to get their duty assignments. After the stunt Lloyd pulled, none of them were in the mood to talk, especially not Ashley.

"Airman First Class Taylor," the red rope called, walking toward her and handing her a slip of paper. "Airman First Class Jefferson," she continued and then walked over to Jefferson. Both girls reviewed their paper and smiled.

"Airman Basic Collier and Airman Basic Grant," she read off again. Both girls raised their hand. "Here you go." She handed them their assignments.

"So what's the verdict?" Lisa asked.

"Andrews Air Force Base." Monique read the paper with a wide smile. "Maryland baby!"

"Langley? Isn't that in Virginia?" Ashley questioned.

"Dillan? Where is Delaware?" Anita was disappointed at the base written on the piece of paper in her hand.

"I got Dillan too." Lisa grinned. It was refreshing to know her new friends would be close by. It was hard to make and keep friends in the military. One minute you're together and the next you were sent someplace else to start all over again.

"Looks like I can't get away from y'all." Ashley finally cracked a smile.

"Oh, don't even act like that. Just be glad you got your sisters to help you with that baby." Lisa rubbed her belly.

"I'm terminating the pregnancy," she mumbled.

Everyone sat in silence, staring at Ashley, who avoided eye contact.

"Are you sure?" Anita asked. Ashley nodded her head. "When . . ." She paused and then thought for a moment "You know what, don't worry. I'll be there with you."

Ashley forced a smile.

They walked out of the Eagle's Nest and headed back to the dorms. Ashley jumped on her cell phone and called around for abortion clinics. Lisa sat on her bed staring out the window. All she could think about was Jerry, what he was doing, and where he could be. He took frequent emergency trips during the week for days at a time. Thoughts of him being with a wife or girlfriend came to her mind. Her thoughts were interrupted when Ashley entered her room. Judging by the puffiness in her eyes, Lisa could tell she had been crying again.

"So when is the day?" Lisa asked, extending her hand to her friend.

"Saturday." She shook her head. "You know why it hurts so badly?" she asked between tears. "This came out of nowhere; there were no signs, no pictures, and no phone calls." She sighed. "Just yesterday we were cuddling, making plans with the new baby." Ashley paused for a moment, shaking her head in disgust. "A marriage."

For the first time, there was nothing Lisa could say or do to comfort her friend. Her tongue was frozen. There were no words that could express her grief or sadness. A part of her felt angry at the idea of a man betraying a woman he claimed to love so deeply. How could someone carry on the charades of a relationship knowing he had someone else waiting for him at home? Sadly, Ashley wasn't the first, and she sure enough wouldn't be the last.

"After all this time, he carried on this relationship like I was the only woman in the world. And all the while he had a wife sitting at home. He's probably making love to her right now, feeding her the same lines he fed me." Ashley walked over to the window. "And this ring, with this ring he proposed to me in front of all my friends. I'm sitting here bragging to my mother and father about a marriage and a baby. I can't even face them, Collier. All they are going to do is say I told you so." Her tears were coming full speed. "I have four sisters, all of them pregnant before the age of eighteen. I made my parents proud when I left the house after high school. The last thing my dad said to me was he was so proud I didn't let some young man come in and destroy my life. Now what do I tell them?" She took the ring off her finger and threw it into the garbage and then turned to Lisa. "Watch yourself. Don't let Jerry do the same to you."

October 26, 2002

Saturday finally came. Lisa, Monique, Ashley, and Anita stood in front of the women's clinic in downtown San Antonio. Ashley squeezed Lisa's hand while the three led her into the building.

"It's going to be okay. I'm here with you," Lisa whispered to an anxious Ashley.

All of them waited in the waiting room for Ashley's name to be called. Her eyes were glassy from crying, and her hair was out of place. This wasn't the Ashley they were used to. Lisa envisioned herself in the same chair waiting for her name to be called. She thought about Jerry and knew that if push came to shove, he wouldn't have been there either. Jerry insisted the relationship was over. He allowed his pride to destroy everything, and now she thought back to the pains in her stomach. If she was pregnant, the baby would have no father.

"Ashley Taylor." A nurse stood behind two double doors, signaling it was time for her exam.

Ashley stared at the nurse as if she'd called the wrong person. *Is this a mistake I will regret?* she wondered. She slowly stood up and walked toward the doors.

"Ma'am, can one of my friends come with me?" Ashley asked. Her voice was low and raspy.

"We don't allow anyone in there except for doctors and medical assistants," she replied.

"Please, ma'am, I can't do this alone." She sobbed uncontrollably.

The nurse watched her for a brief moment and then signaled Ashley to hold on for a moment. When she returned, the nurse nodded her head. Ashley turned to Anita and motioned for her to come with her. She jumped to her feet and immediately ran to Ashley. The nurse pulled Anita to the side and gave her strict step-by-step instructions while Ashley prepped.

Anita entered the room and stared at Ashley, who was stretched across the bed with her arms tied down. She'd been shaking so hard the medical assistant had been unable to give her any fluids or anesthesia. She had an oxygen mask on her face, and tears were falling down her cheeks. Anita pulled her chair close to her, holding her hand.

"This operation will be quick, so we need her calm while we administer the anesthesia. We prefer you concentrate on your friend and avoid asking any questions," the medical assistant said sternly.

Anita nodded her head and directed her attention toward Ashley, who'd already begun to feel woozy. In less than a minute, she was asleep. Anita picked up the napkin and wiped her friend's face. Just as the MA had said, the procedure was quick—only five minutes. After they cleaned Ashley up, Anita was escorted back to the lobby, while Ashley was wheeled to the recovery room.

"How did she do?" Monique asked.

Anita gave a slight smile. "My girl's a trooper." Her smiled faded, and then she sat down in her chair.

Monique grabbed her phone and opened it to answer her call. The look on her face told Anita it was bad news.

"Grant, what's wrong?" asked Anita.

She closed her phone and then turned toward the direction Lisa was sitting. Lisa didn't bother to look up; she just continued playing with the ring on her finger. The worried look on Monique's face caught her off guard, and she knew the bad news was about her.

"What is it?" Lisa's voice cracked.

Monique kneeled in front of her and then grabbed her hands.

"That was Williams. He said Jerry is back in Killeen. His unit is scheduled to deploy in the next few weeks." Lisa kept quiet. She couldn't bring herself to say anything; all she could do was cry. The vibration of her phone startled her, and she jumped to answer.

"Hello?" Her voice cracked.

"Is this Airman Collier?" the unfamiliar voice asked.

"Yes, this is her." She wiped her face.

"This is Captain Donovan from Wilson Hall. You had your physical earlier this week. We took a pregnancy test, and it came back positive. Do your training leaders know about this?" the voice questioned.

Unable to respond she slowly closed her cell phone and stuffed it back in her pocket. The news of Jerry and pregnancy at the same time put her in a state of shock. Many thoughts roamed in her mind but there was only one question she could muster.

"When do they deploy Grant?" Lisa's eyes were glossy but she refused to cry.

"He said a couple of weeks. He's on his way back to Hood now, and then it's off to Camp Anaconda." Monique eyed her down. "Look, we're going to get through this, okay?" She reached up and gave her a hug. Lisa ignored her, drowned in her own thoughts. Even though she wasn't prepared to go through it alone, she wasn't prepared to be with Jerry while he was deployed. In his world, he was moving on. *Well, baby, it looks as though it's just you and me.*

CHAPTER 9

First Duty Station

November 18, 2002

Two weeks of first-term airman's classes and briefings, Lisa and Anita were finally settled at their new base. The pregnancy was just starting to take its toll on Lisa, while Anita was ready to find her Mr. Right and settle down. Justin was a good man, but she refused to entertain a long distance relationship. After expressing her concerns over a text message, Anita ended the six-week relationship with a single "good-bye." The last she heard, he continued on to his new base with a new attitude and a new girl.

Full of energy and ready to work, Anita power walked toward her new place of employment. Lisa dragged behind her.

"Come on, girl, we only got ten minutes before were supposed to meet up with our supervisor," Anita screamed, stuffing her paperwork into her book bag.

"How much further? I'm tired," Lisa screamed from behind, out of breath.

"There." Anita pointed to the long building located next to the south gate.

By the time Lisa caught up to Anita, she was already walking through the double doors. The moment Anita walked in, she scanned every available man who passed her. A few had potential but were already taken, with wedding rings strapped tightly to their fingers.

"All right, where are we going?" Lisa knelt over, trying to catch her breath. Her stomach ached from hunger.

Anita ignored her as she read the signs for the warehouse. A passerby quickly stopped when he noticed the two clueless young airmen.

"Can I help you?" the young lieutenant asked.

"Yes." She smiled at the handsome man standing in front of her. "We're looking for building 239. I think we may be a little lost."

"Well, you are in building 239. Now the real question is, where you headed to?" He smiled as wide as he could.

"The warehouse," Lisa blurted, standing back to her feet and adjusting her uniform.

"You okay?" he questioned, staring at Lisa, who appeared distraught.

"She's fine," Anita intervened. "Yes, we are looking for the warehouse. We're new here, and neither one of us has a clue as to where we're going or what we're doing."

"Ah, I see. Just follow the steps through the double doors and keep walking until you see a cage. Bang on the door, and they'll let you in." He pointed to a small staircase behind him. Anita smiled sweetly, and then pulled her friend towards the doors. The Lieutenant watched as both women walked away.

Upon entering the gate, there were three offices located to their immediate left. On the right was the open bay leading to the bin rows. Toward the opposite direction of the bay were two rolling doors exiting to the parking lot. This allowed trucks to load and unload deliveries. Anita paid close attention to a few gentlemen standing at one of the openings, but none of them caught her interest. She quickly ducked her head into the office labelled "Storage and Issue." A gray-haired master sergeant greeted the women with a smile and directed them to their assignments. Following their meet and greet with their new supervisor, the girls jetted through the rolling doors and out into the parking lot toward the chow hall. Lucky for them, Dillan was small enough they could walk to and from their destinations. The base consisted of one main road leading from one gate to another with shopping centers and office buildings in between. Unfortunately for Lisa, that meant more pressure on her feet. The women followed a crowd of airmen walking into the chow hall located in front of the dormitories.

"I can't believe we have been here for over two weeks, gone on three tours, and we have yet to find a decent-looking, single man," Anita blurted out.

"If you put more focus in getting us a car as you do in finding a man we could get somewhere," Lisa responded, rubbing her already eight-weeks-pregnant belly.

"How is the pregnancy going?" Anita asked while grabbing her tray and utensils. Almost every chow hall in the air force was the same. Once you walked through the double doors, there was seating on your left and right. By the time you reached the food line, you had an option of fast food or real food. It was the same for breakfast, lunch, dinner, and midnight chow.

"The pregnancy is going okay, considering I'm alone, I'm sleeping in a twin bed, and I share my bathroom with another chick I don't even know." She took a deep breath and then continued. "I guess it's good. Eventually my suite mate is going to get irritated with me throwing up in the bathroom every morning."

"They won't give you anything for the nausea?"

"Nope, they said it's normal."

"Has Jerry made any attempt to contact you?"

"Nope, and he's not going to. I don't have any of his friends' numbers, and he doesn't talk to any of mine." Lisa scanned the buffet line for anything remotely normal enough to eat.

"They got anything good?" Anita eyed the menu.

"If you're looking for something good, then the chow hall is not the place to be," The tall, handsome figure turned to look at Anita, who had been standing in front of them the entire time.

"You?" She smiled at the lieutenant.

"I thought that voice sounded familiar." His sparkling green eyes gazed into hers. She stood silent for a moment, hypnotized by the beautiful man. She scanned his uniform for his name and then remembered she was speaking to an officer.

"Oh, I'm sorry, First Lieutenant . . . uh . . . Brooks." She cleared her throat at the disappointment.

He smiled. "It's okay, and please call me Brandon. First Lieutenant Brooks is so official. I'm just an average joe."

She laughed at his cockiness. Too bad officer and enlistment relationships were against the rules or else she would have jumped on this ride from the first hello.

"Where are you sitting?" he pondered aloud.

"I guess over by the big screen." She pointed to the TV in the middle section of the room.

"Good spot." He nodded. "I guess I'll see you around."

Lisa and Anita grabbed their food and headed for an available booth closest to the television. Anita noticed Lieutenant Brooks sitting nearby. She laughed at herself for being so silly. The idea of a relationship or fling with him was merely wishful thinking. When she caught a glimpse of him staring her way, she acknowledged his stare with a smile.

"I don't know what it is about him, but he is so gorgeous," Anita blurted out in midconversation, throwing Lisa completely off guard.

"Huh?" she questioned, and then she followed the direction Anita was staring. "Who, that first lieutenant?"

"Sadly, yes." She sighed.

"Nita, say these words with me: fraternization and UCMJ. He is brass, you are stripes, and the two do not mix in the military world. Plus, he's not just a lieutenant; he's a *first* lieutenant, meaning he could be putting captain on any day now. Way above your league, girlfriend," Lisa said, attempting to speak sense into Anita, but she wasn't listening. "Hello, Earth to Nita J." She waved her hand in front of her face.

"What? It's just harmless flirting. What's wrong with that?" She played innocent.

"Everything." Lisa's tone was serious. "Nita, he is not just flirting with you. Those eyes staring at you right now are telling me that he wants something from you. And it ain't your french fries on your tray." Lisa rolled her eyes.

"Hush girl—he's coming over." Anita adjusted herself nonchalantly, turning her attention back to Lisa.

Brandon casually walked over to their table. He handed Anita a piece of paper, placing it directly onto her lap. He looked up at Lisa, whose facial expression wore a harsh frown. He respectfully nodded to avoid making any scenes that would attract unwanted attention. Anita grabbed the paper and then stuffed it into her side pocket while the lieutenant headed for the exit. Lisa rolled her eyes at her friend and continued eating her food. Anita smiled widely, unfolding the paper, anxious to read what was written.

> *Hello, beautiful. I hope I'm not out of line. Let me first start out by saying you are a very attractive woman. I hope I can see more of you. If you are interested, call me at 555-9283. I play football for our squadron. Hope you come out and see me in action. I think you might like what you see.*
>
> *Brandon*

November 20, 2002

"Oh, my goodness, I'm so si—" Lisa could barely finish her sentence, she was already throwing up.

"You need to get better because we are going to Brandon's game tonight," Anita stated while holding Lisa's hair and rubbing her back.

"I'll be okay. Just give me a min—" Lisa reached for the toilet paper, trying to wipe her mouth.

After praising the porcelain goddess for what seemed to be an eternity, she changed out of her uniform into a denim short set and matching t-shirt. She viewed her reflection, cringing at the idea that her flat abdomen would soon be just a faded memory.

The football field was located directly in front of the security forces building. It wasn't much to look at, considering it was merely a track used for physical training testing. There were people seated from every angle waiting for their squadron to play. Lisa took a seat at the end of the bleachers, not noticing the gentleman sitting three steps up. He admired her as soon as he saw her from the parking lot. Anita looked around for Brandon and then took her seat beside Lisa. Brian was in the same unit as both of them and had his eye on Lisa since the first day she arrived. He would see her daily, hoping to get enough courage to talk to her, praying she hadn't heard anything about his reputation. He and his friends Deon, Mark, and Devon were notorious around Dillan Air Force Base as being playboys and problem children, throwing wild parties and other mischievous activities.

"S'up, Collier? You look nice this evening." He eyed her from head to toe.

"Roberts, right?" Lisa ignored him, trying not to make eye contact. He smiled.

"Call me Brian." Lisa didn't respond.

"Hey, Roberts, you work the part store, right?" Anita asked, interrupting the one-man conversation.

"Yes ma'am. I'm sorry I never got a chance to talk to you at work, but you know how hectic it is." His eyes were fixed on Lisa.

"It's okay, I'm not that friendly anyway," Lisa responded, hoping he'd get the idea she wasn't interested in any kind of conversation.

Anita laughed, shaking her head.

"Good, because I am." He laughed. Lisa rolled her eyes. She'd overheard the girls at her job talk about Brian and his friends. The last thing she was going to do was get involved with another Jerry situation.

The game between the Logistics Readiness Squadron and the Civil Engineer Squadron was just about to begin. Anita was on the edge of her seat, waiting to get a glimpse of Brandon in action. She watched as he ran across the field, splitting between two of the opposing team members with ease. He was a beautiful sight to see, but most of all, he had money and power. Silently she prayed this would be her Mr. Right. She'd had too many disappointments; it was time for something real. After scoring a touchdown, he ran to his teammates, coaching them on the next play. Anita enjoyed watching him take charge. When he noticed her watching him, he smiled gratefully at the young beauty coming to support him. Brian hollered when a team member scored the winning touchdown.

"That's right, LRS!" he screamed across the field.

"Is that necessary?" Lisa retorted.

"Just happy for my team." He smiled.

"Then maybe you should be on the field playing." She rolled her eyes.

"I was playing, but I banged my knee pretty badly." He lifted his shorts, exposing his injury. She didn't bother to turn around. "I was the best running back out of every team on this base," he continued, but she refused to look back in his direction.

"And now you're sitting here bothering me," she said sarcastically. Anita laughed at her friend's rude behavior.

"Girl, lighten up. Brian, walk with me to congratulate the team." Anita didn't wait for a response. Lisa just rolled her eyes.

As soon as the game was over, Anita ran over to Brandon. She knew she had to play it cool, so she nonchalantly congratulated each team member. Brandon walked over to Anita and shook her hand. He slipped another letter in her hand and walked away. She opened it as fast as she could.

I knew you'd show. Meet you at the dorms tonight at nine. I promise you won't regret it.

Brandon

She looked down at her watch and saw it was already eight o'clock. This would give her enough time to walk Lisa back to the dorm, get in the shower, and then slip on something sexy. She searched around the field for Lisa, who was sitting with a coworker, Jasmine. Jasmine was Hispanic, with long brown hair and brown eyes. She was very beautiful and could have had anyone she'd wanted. Sadly her heart belonged to the biggest play boy on the base, Deon. He was a man who was known for having different women around.

"S'up, senorita?" Anita sang.

"Hey, Nita. I see you checking the players out. So give it up, which one?" Jasmine asked curiously.

"Reyes, as much as I tolerate you, my business is still my business," Anita joked.

"In other words, he's probably somebody you don't have any business messing with!" She laughed. "Anyway, on that note, I'll change the subject. Are you all going to Deon's party Friday night?"

"I don't think so," Lisa said casually.

"Yes, *we* are." Anita poked Lisa's shoulder.

"Great" Jasmine smiled.

"I am not going to some party. In case you forgot, I'm pregnant. Plus I don't like Deon or his stupid friends," Lisa snapped.

"You really sound like a nine-year-old right now, and from what I hear Brian is a nice guy. You should give him a chance," Jasmine pleaded.

"Did you not hear me when I said I'm pregnant?" Lisa said slowly as if Jasmine could not understand.

"Yes, I did, but you aren't even showing yet, so get up and have some fun with your friends before you are too big you won't be able to walk out the door." Jasmine laughed.

"That's funny to you?" Lisa snapped.

"Hey, can we wrap this up? I have some place to be in an hour," Anita chimed in.

"And where do you have to be late in the evening on a work night?" asked Lisa.

"Mom, I'll be back before curfew, don't trip." She grabbed the two women by their arms and headed towards Jasmine's car. She dropped the girls off then headed towards her apartment off base.

Once the girls arrived back to the dorms, Anita was already storming to her room. She couldn't wait to see what Brandon had in store for her. Brandon was almost too good to be true. Not only was he going to be her man, but he was also going to be a means to an end. She threw all of her dresses onto the floor, picking out all the ones that were either too long or not revealing enough. A black lace number sitting isolated on the floor was the perfect dress to impress the first lieutenant. The sheer fabric fit around each curve just enough to expose the beautiful, toned body the BDUs tried so hard to cover. Her heels were high, making her legs longer and more desirable. She ran down the steps to the parking lot, waiting for her knight to arrive. Just as promised, he pulled up in his Mercedes BMW at nine o'clock on the dot. She eyed the car as if it were made of pure gold.

"Hello, beautiful." He slid out of the car and gave her a hug. The embrace was just what she needed. He placed the keys in her hand and motioned for her to get in.

"Me? You trust me to drive your car?" she questioned.

"You have your license, correct?" He laughed. "Can you drive?"

"Yes and yes, but this is a Mercedes," she responded. "Give me a regular four door with wheels and I'm cool, but this is an expensive car."

"Be careful and don't crash." He walked over to the passenger side. Her expression gave him the notion she was impressed. When she turned the ignition, the car purred like a kitten. She pulled out of the parking lot and then headed for the north gate exit.

"So where are we going?" She couldn't take her eyes of the detailed interior.

"Just follow my directions and you'll see," he instructed. "And watch the road; this won't be the last time you're in my car." Young women were his preference because they were easy to please. A flash of a smile and some money and they would do almost anything he commanded.

He directed her toward a wooded area. The dimly lit passage could've been a gateway to anywhere. She silently prayed he wasn't a secret serial rapist trapping her into his master plan. They exited the car, passing the "Do Not Enter" sign; he covered her eyes and escorted her to the sound of running water. When he uncovered her eyes, she could see an image of what appeared to be a small waterfall. The moon and stars were at their brightest.

"Wow." She gasped at the beautiful sight.

"The best is yet to come." He smiled as he signaled her to stay put while he ran back to the car. She was so intrigued by the beauty of nature. The glare from the moon bounced off of the dark, mysterious river. When Brandon returned, he had a bottle, a blanket, and two wine glasses in his hand. She embraced him with a hug while he used this opportunity to work his way and feel what he'd been eyeing the entire time in the car.

"How do you know about this place?" She loosened her grip from around his neck.

"I come out here to fish." He pointed to the river.

"Oh, you fish?"

"Yeah, but I won't eat anything I catch. This water is so polluted you'll find yourself in the hospital getting all types of vaccinations." He laughed.

"So, Mr. Brandon, I'm going to warn you: I'm looking for something serious."

"Okay." He cleared his throat. "So are you asking me to be your boyfriend?"

"Look, I may be bold enough to speak on what I want, but I'm still old fashioned and prefer a man to ask me out."

"Okay, this is what I'll do. I'll write on a little note and ask you out. Will that work?" he joked.

"I'll save you the paper. How about I just say yes?" She giggled.

CHAPTER 10

First Night Out

November 23, 2002

*I*n their first week as career women, Lisa could not believe how fast paced the military was. School did not prepare her for the long hours she would spend in the warehouse. Every time she turned around maintenance personnel were calling for parts and pieces to fix an aircraft waiting to fly out to overseas locations. In some cases, personnel were called in the middle of the night to come in and deliver parts directly to the aircraft. It was a long and exhausting week and Friday was finally here, which meant it was time to bring out the tight-fitting dresses and six-inch heels. Everyone in the squadron bragged about the upcoming party off base. These parties were rarely ever empty, and in most cases, they always ended with the police knocking on the door. This only excited the young people to attend more parties. Lisa, as usual, had been throwing up all day. She knew there was no way of backing out of tonight's festivities. Anita would've dragged her by her hair and stuffed some Tums down her throat just to ease her stomach long enough to get her to dance to a couple of songs. As Jasmine mentioned, she was waiting outside the door at 7:00 p.m. Anita texted Brandon to meet them at Deon's house. She'd been spending every day that week with him in the same spot. That was the only place they could be together without anyone seeing them or asking any questions. As much as Anita loved Mother Nature, it was time to upgrade to a hotel. She became fed up with the outside fantasy after finding a couple of leaves in her shoes and twig imprints on her back. Lisa finally made her way out of the bathroom, where she spotted Anita adjusting her hair in the mirror.

"Hey" Anita paused for a moment to greet her sickly friend.

"Hey." Lisa wiped the edges of her mouth. "I just got a text from Monique. She said she's driving up from Andrews."

"Great, how long will it be before she gets up here?"

"She told me she was on her way almost an hour ago."

"Good, it'll be like old times. Too bad Ashley couldn't make it." Anita sighed. After the abortion in Texas, they had all parted ways, and she hadn't talked to Ashley since. "Have you talked to her?"

"She changed her number. Monique said she hasn't heard from her either," Lisa said while brushing her teeth.

"Come on, I'm out here blasting my music, waking up your neighbors. I had a rough week. I'm ready to get to this party." Jasmine burst into the room.

"What neighbors? We live in the dorms. These people are not asleep!" Anita shouted from the bathroom.

"Are you two done yet?" Jasmine rolled her eyes.

"Almost." Lisa wiped her mouth.

"Please tell me you're going to the doctor's on Monday. You look like crap," Jasmine hollered.

"No one asked you!" Lisa snapped as she grabbed her things and headed out the door.

As usual, the party was packed and loud. The crowd spilled from every opening in the house. People from all over the base were in attendance. Deon and his roommates were known for throwing some of the best parties in town. Anybody who was anybody was there flashing off their cars and money. Jasmine spotted Deon on the porch with Mark, Devon, and Brian playing cards. She couldn't wait for him to see her in her new dress.

Normally their flirting consisted of a few stares and smiles, but tonight she was ready to take it to a new level. Unfortunately, she was so determined for him to notice her, she missed the young lady standing over his shoulder. The young beauty looked like a model to the untrained eye. No one would have ever expected her to be in the military.

"Hey, Deon," Jasmine flirted. The woman glared at Deon's beautiful desperate fan.

"Hey, Jas." He smiled and then turned his attention back to his game. The young woman didn't appreciate her stares going unnoticed.

"Hello, I'm Natalie," the overly covetous woman interrupted.

Natalie had many run-ins with Deon's women in the past, but she could never be defeated. Although Deon enjoyed the company of different women, oddly enough he had a soft spot for her only. She fought long and hard for her romance and no one was capable of filling her shoes, especially not an enlisted member. Natalie was a butter bar—a second lieutenant—which meant she was in a powerful position. Unlike many of her peers, Natalie came into the military through ROTC in college. She was only 23 years old and completely naïve when it came to the consequences when breaking military rules. In her mind she felt as long as she never got caught she could do whatever she wanted, which included dating enlisted men. Most of the men in the officer world were much older than her, and her choices of a compatible mate were very limited.

Jasmine ignored the unruly woman and focused her attention back to Deon. "You going to save me a dance?" she continued.

"Wow, I see you just didn't catch the hint the first time," Natalie joked.

"Can I help you?" Jasmine asked, frustrated.

"Deon is mine. I don't appreciate women disrespecting me, thinking he's going to give them two minutes of his time because they decided not to put any clothes on," Natalie spat, moving closer to Jasmine.

"Your women are messing with my concentration," Mark blurted.

"Don't put it on them, you were losing anyway." Deon laughed carelessly.

"Deon, your fan club is just getting outrageous, aren't they?" Natalie snapped.

Deon jumped on his feet and then separated the two women. Jasmine couldn't believe how calm he was acting or the fact some woman she didn't even know was trying to disrespect her over him. Even though she liked Deon, it became personal when Natalie tried to insult her in front of a crowd of people.

"You know what? I'm going to find my friends. De, I hope I get to see you later," Jasmine whispered in his ear while she gave him a long hug. She turned her attention to Natalie and then rolled her eyes. "I'm sorry, what was your name?"

Natalie was ready to leap across and scratch Jasmine's eyes out "My name is Natalie!" she growled.

"Natalie?" Jasmine repeated. "It was nice meeting you. Oh, by the way, I love that outfit." She turned to walk away.

"Oh, you funny, tramp!" Natalie snapped.

Jasmine refused to give Natalie's insult a second thought. She turned away gracefully, holding her head high as the victorious one. Her mission was to find her friends. When she made her way through the door, she found Lisa with her back against the wall, bobbing to the music. She had a cup in her hand and was practically ignoring every man in the building. Jasmine laughed at her friend for being so rude. Lisa spotted Jasmine smiling from ear to ear.

"Where have you been?" Lisa said while taking a sip of her ginger ale.

"Visiting the man of my dreams," she winked. "Come to find out his little pit bull isn't too fond of me." Jasmine laughed at her encounter with Natalie. "She tried to get a little disrespectful out there."

"Huh?"

"I guess he has a girlfriend."

"Be careful." She sipped her soda before speaking again. "So why is that fool Brian following me around? He's like a shadow—every time I turn around, he's right there staring at me." Lisa shook her head. Brian's persistence was almost as bad as Jerry's.

"Why won't you talk to him? He's a nice guy from what I hear." Anita chimed in to the conversation from behind.

"Nita, did we not have this same conversation about Jerry?" Lisa whined.

"Yes, but we are talking about two different people. Who's to say Brian is the same way?" Jasmine defended.

"Whatever, the last time I took somebody's relationship advice, I ended up eight weeks pregnant with a boyfriend who left town with no number or contact, and oh, yeah, who is now ducking and dodging bullets in a foreign country . . . Um, let me think . . . Nope. I ain't listening to anyone anymore," Lisa ranted.

"Seek therapy, girlfriend." Anita laughed.

Lisa's hormones were making her insane. At times she was difficult to talk to. No one knew what to expect. One moment Lisa was the sweetest and the next she was ready to slice you from ear to ear. They continued the evening in the corner. Lisa felt her cell phone vibrate and quickly answered when she recognized Monique's numbers. She ran through the front door to greet her buddy.

"Mo!" Lisa yelled excitingly.

"Hey, beautiful, I see you still got the flat stomach going. How much longer before I see a bump?" She rubbed Lisa's belly.

"Well . . ." she began.

"Monique, thank goodness you're here. I thought we were going to have to take Collier out. She's been snapping on everyone," Anita joked, giving her best friend a high five. Monique chuckled to herself and then cleared her throat when she noticed the evil face Lisa was making at the both of them.

"Let the party begin." Monique pointed to the front door. They passed a group of onlookers, eager to watch the women strut their stuff. The four beauties were like a powerful force, ready to take down and break down anything or anyone standing in their way. The attention they got at the party put them in the limelight. This was exactly what Jasmine needed to hook her man in her plan. She needed him to see that she was a catch and he'd be a fool not to take what many other men wanted. The four maneuvered around the house, dancing and partying without a care in the world. Three songs later, Anita spotted Brandon. She quickly ran to him, attempting to kiss him.

"You know we can't be seen, Anita. There are too many eyes out here," he warned.

"Who cares?" She pouted.

"Do you want me to get into trouble?" He sighed.

"No, but I want you tonight. Can't we get a hotel or something?" she whined.

"I got something better. We can go to my house; I want you for the entire weekend." He pulled her outside toward his car, which was parked secluded from the others. She looked around, making sure no one spotted her jumping into his car. The crowd gathered on the porch was already past its alcohol limit and barely noticed them speed away.

Deon had been watching Jasmine the entire night. He wanted her bad, and this was definitely the time to put his plan into action. He walked over to Devon, who was entertaining a young girl from the Medical Squadron. She wasn't much to look at, but with all the alcohol in his system, he couldn't tell the difference.

"Yo, Dev," Deon interrupted.

"Hey man?" Devon turned to his friend with glassy eyes.

"Hey, I'm about to take Jasmine to the room. You know the routine." Deon grinned.

"Cool. I'll set up the equipment." Devon excused himself from his bait.

He quickly leaped up the steps into the bedroom. The tape recorder was displayed on the closet shelf, pointing directly onto Deon's bed. He switched the on button and hurried out of the room before Jasmine noticed anything strange. They recorded women performing sexual acts and showed them to their peers on base. In most cases, the woman would never know. To the outside world, they were heartless, but it was never personal, just entertaining. Deon enjoyed the freedom of life. After his first heartbreak in elementary school he vowed to never get close to women again. Born and raised in Orlando Florida, he was no stranger to the party life style. His family was originally from Barbados, and came to America seeking wealthy opportunities. He along with his four brothers were ruthless trouble makers growing up in and out of the detention centers. Deon's father forced him to volunteer for military service or else he would spend the rest of his life in jail.

Mark was a different animal. He grew up in Los Angeles and knew the drug game like a game of chess. He and a childhood friend, Mike, grew up representing a notorious street gang for eleven years. They were hit men for a drug lord by the name of Tony B. By the age of nineteen, Mark was making more money than anyone in his neighborhood combined. Life was great until Mike and Tony B were gunned down right before his very own eyes over a drug deal that went bad. He ran away, hoping to escape the life of violence, only to find shelter at the nearest recruiting station. All he wanted to do was sign on the dotted line and get out of Los Angeles. With no previous conviction on record or dependents to care for, the enlistment process was fast and easy. Mark's determination to leave the city he knew all too well landed him in Lackland Air Force Base for basic training less than three weeks later.

Devon came from a struggling single mother. All he ever seen was his mother push and save for him and his little sister. They were pretty close until his mother remarried a man who would later become Devon's worst nightmare. His new stepfather started drinking after losing his job and then turned to beating on

Devon's mother. Devon came home one day to find his mother on the floor while his stepfather beat her over and over again. Devon ran to her aid, and instead of being grateful, she kicked him out so her new husband wouldn't leave.

Brian came from a strong, wealthy family, never got involved with gangs, and had never seen crack or cocaine outside of the movies. Brian's issue wasn't internal; it was external. When he was a baby, his father got into a car accident. The glass from the window shattered, causing a major gash above his right eye. The scar never healed, giving him the nickname "Scarface" in school. His eye was slightly damaged but still functional. He was good looking, but the scar and damage to his eye made him stand out from the other children. When he joined the military, he had his own money and bought his own car. He figured if he couldn't get women with his looks, money was the next best thing. Once he became friends with Mark and Deon, his reputation went through the roof. He could have almost any woman he wanted, if he tried hard enough. Unlike his friends, he never believed in disrespecting women. He was always a one woman man, never entertained the idea of casual dating.

As far as the night went, Brian was on a mission to get Lisa. He wanted her and figured if he was going to get her, he had to move quickly. She was a good-looking girl, so it wouldn't be hard for another man to step and get hired before he could even put in an application. Deon was working his magic with Jasmine, and they were already headed for the stairs. When Lisa noticed Brian, she rolled her eyes. Monique turned to see what Lisa was looking at.

"Hello, Miss." Brian smiled, showing off his pearly whites.

"Brian, isn't there someone else you could be harassing?" She rolled her eyes and then walked away.

"Collier, wait up," Monique called after before turning her attention to Brian. "Sorry, she's pregnant, so her hormones are all out of control," Monique explained before chasing after her.

"Pregnant?" whispered Brian. *No wonder*. He sighed with disappointment.

Monique chased Lisa to the porch, where they spotted Natalie cursing at Devon. The two women were not too comfortable with Natalie's tone and knew something was wrong. She had her cell phone in her hand calling for her back up while loudly plotting on "the low-life tramp." When Natalie described the vixen, Lisa knew she was referring to Jasmine.

"I already know what's going on, so stop playing games with me!" she screamed to whoever was on the phone.

"Is she talking about Jasmine?" Monique asked.

"Yeah," Lisa mumbled and then ran into the house and up the stairs to find her friend before it was too late. She kicked open the door and saw Deon and Jasmine in the bed. To her surprise, Natalie was right behind her, and Monique wasn't too far. Jasmine swiftly ran for her clothes while Deon calmly grabbed a handful of his jeans and adjusted his clothes.

"You cannot possibly be this stupid," Natalie said while walking toward Jasmine.

"What are you talking about?" Jasmine asked while adjusting her dressed.

"You are so desperate!" Natalie leaped toward Jasmine. Deon didn't say a word. He casually stepped out of the way so the women could argue.

"Who are you talking to?" Jasmine pushed Natalie out of her face.

"No, leave her alone!" Monique jumped and blocked Jasmine from Natalie's grasp.

Lisa, Monique, and Jasmine were cornered in the room by Natalie and four of her friends. Deon ran downstairs and grabbed Mark to come see the dispute.

"Hey, Mark, the girls are about to fight," Deon said proudly.

"Is the camera still on?" Mark responded while the two men flew up the steps to watch the action.

"We didn't come here to fight," Lisa pleaded. Two of Natalie's friends approached her, but Lisa refused to show fear. She stood her ground, waiting for one of them to make a move.

"Well, we did," said one of the girls.

"No, you guys don't have to fight. But I'm going to teach this one a lesson about messing with other women's men." Natalie extended her hand, grabbing Jasmine's hair. Monique moved out of the way to avoid contact. Jasmine and Natalie sprang into combat. Natalie pulled Jasmine's hair while Jasmine pushed her away. Monique grabbed for Jasmine, trying to break the two up. Lisa pulled out her cell phone. One of the other women knocked her to the floor and snatched her phone away. She grabbed one of Deon's boots on the floor and swung it at the girl. The girl fell to the floor from the blow to her leg. Monique broke away from Jasmine to help Lisa. Natalie's other two friends quickly grabbed Monique and held her down. Lisa sprung from the floor and swung the boot at one of the women. Monique broke free and pulled Natalie off of Jasmine. She was on the floor moaning in pain. Lisa grabbed her phone and called 911 while Deon and Mark critiqued the brawl.

"So Mark, who do you think will be today's championship winner?" Deon laughed while motioning an imaginary microphone to Mark.

"You know what, Deon, it's a close call between Natalie and the unknown woman punching her in the throat." Mark referred to Monique.

Lisa stuffed her phone back into her pocket and then grabbed Monique away from Natalie. Jasmine pulled out her mace and sprayed to one of the women huddling over her. She screamed, grabbing her eyes, and backed away. The fumes from the spray spread heavily throughout the room, causing people to choke and cough. Brian grabbed Lisa from behind and dragged her out of the room. Everyone else ran for the stairwell to avoid any kind of exposure. Brian continued to drag Lisa, pulling her down the stairs while she coughed and screamed hysterically. The crowd watched in horror. She tried to claw into Brian's arm, hoping he would let her go. He dragged her through the front door to his car and stuffed her in the backseat. She attempted to grab the handle, but he managed to switch on the child safety lock. The only way she was going to be able to get out of the car was if she climbed through the front. He jumped into the driver side and started the car.

"Let me go, Brian. One of them kicked me in the stomach." She yanked the door handle, but it wouldn't budge. Blue and red lights shined brightly from behind, and Lisa slouched back into the seat. Policemen ran through the crowd into the home, forcing everyone to vacate the premises. Brian watched carefully until the cops were no longer in sight.

"Look, right now you are upset, so you aren't thinking clearly. If you don't chill out, you are going to lose that baby. Cops are here, and I'm sure you're not trying to go to prison in your condition," he lectured. She decided to comply with his demands. He slowly backed away to avoid any attention, and once the coast was clear, he sped off.

"How did you know I was pregnant?" She rolled her eyes.

"Does it matter?" he questioned, never taking his eyes off of the road.

"Why do you care, anyway? I saw your friends up there. You're probably just like them."

"I am nothing like them. Be thankful I got you out of there before something really bad happened to you."

"Well, if you are looking for a thank-you, you can forget it." She crossed her arms.

"You haven't been nice to me yet, so I don't expect anything from you." He laughed.

She thought for a moment and then realized he was right. Jerry had burned her so badly she had never realized how her behavior toward men had soured. Deep down she wanted every man to pay for the pain she was in. The heartbreak from Jerry was still as painful as the day he left her standing in front of the dorms.

"Look, my intentions were never against you. I have some emotions inside of me, it's nothing personal." She was looking out the window at the oncoming traffic while he observed her from the rearview mirror. "It's just a natural reaction, I guess."

"Don't get me wrong, I think you're beautiful. I wouldn't mind a couple of dates here and there." He smiled through the rearview mirror. She avoided eye contact but couldn't help but smile. "Oh, let me guess, you probably like those pretty boys with college degrees, huh?"

She laughed a little. "No, I prefer hardworking men with ambition. You don't have to have a degree, just a plan."

"Oh, so you like, what rough, gang member-type dudes?"

"Where are you taking me?" She changed the subject.

"Back to the base. What dorm are you at?" He waited patiently for the light off the ramp to turn green.

"You can drop me off at the gate; my dorm is not that far." She pointed to the visible dorms closest to the highway.

"Why are you so stubborn? I just want a clear conscience and to know that you made it home safely."

"Why?"

He was trying to think of something to say to open her up a little. He couldn't for the life of him figure out why she was being so tough. All he knew was her last boyfriend was definitely going to make the next one pay big time. He slowly drove toward a shack-looking building and waited for the gate guard.

"Hey, what's up, man?" said the man walking toward Brian's vehicle.

"Hey. I got this crazy female in my backseat. Just picked her up for fighting." He turned to look at Lisa, but she wasn't amused by his jokes.

"Oh." The man nodded and then chuckled to himself. "How was the party?"

"That's where I got this one from. Tell her I am nothing like Mark and Deon. She doesn't believe the sweetheart I really am." Brian pointed at Lisa.

"What is this? Can you please excuse this man so I can get home?" She shot him a dirty look and then turned back to face the window.

"Oh, I know you. You're friends with Williams and Cole, right?" he asked, walking to the backseat window.

"Yeah." She nodded slowly.

"Yeah, I remember you. Do you remember seeing me around?"

She thought hard for a moment and then shook her head. "Do you still talk to Cole?"

"Nope, last time we spoke was about five weeks ago after my graduation. He graduated this week, I think, right?"

"Sounds about right." She smiled.

"It was nice talking to you, Brian. I'll catch you later." He shook Brian's hand and then walked back into the tiny building.

Brian continued driving until he reached the light and then turned back to Lisa.

"Wow, she actually smiles"

She looked at him and then shrugged her shoulders. He shook his head in frustration. The beauty refused to break down her barriers.

"So, um, where do you stay? I can't drive around the base all night. I'm sure one of these cops might get suspicious." He looked around.

"Oh, I'm sorry. I'm at building 445 by the church."

He drove to the instructed site. She quietly exited the car, hoping he wouldn't try to follow her. She gave a slight wave, thanked him for the ride, and then headed for her room. The entire dorm was lifeless, in complete silence. She rushed in, collapsed on her bed, and then opened her phone to call Monique. The phone rang three times before she picked up. After Brian dragged Lisa in the car, Monique pulled Jasmine out of the house into her car and then headed back to Maryland for the weekend while everything cooled down. The police came storming through the doors, forcing everyone to leave the area. Thanks to the massive crowd, they were unable to identify the caller or the other women involved in the dispute. Jasmine had scratches on her face and bruises on her chest and stomach from all the kicking. The worst part of it all was Deon and Mark had it all on film. It was only a matter of time before the videos were released on base. Jasmine made a few phone calls about the mystery woman and came to find not only was she an officer but also a second lieutenant in the same squadron as Deon. *Two strikes!*

CHAPTER 11

Aftermath

November 24, 2002

*J*asmine examined the damage to her face in the mirror. She shook her head, angry at the idea that someone would even violate her in such a way. Monique was sitting on the bed watching television.

"Can you believe this, Grant? They had the nerve to record her attacking me. I bet they are showing those tapes to everyone on base," Jasmine shouted.

"Don't worry by Monday that fight will be just a forgotten memory. Deon isn't dumb enough to put his career in jeopardy." Monique attempted to shine some form of light to the situation. Jasmine was a ticking time bomb ready to explode on Deon and Natalie.

"Well, it's obvious Natalie doesn't care about her career." She walked around Monique's room, reliving the embarrassing moment in her mind. Monique watched her pace back and forth. The noticeable marks on her face extended from the corner of her eye down to her cheekbone.

"Since Deon likes to record," she paused and then looked at Monique with a wide grin from ear to ear, "I wonder how Ms. Natalie's supervisor would feel about her messing around with her subordinate."

"Couldn't we just eat cookie dough and watch chick flicks?" Monique pleaded. Jasmine's plan sounded good, but to actually pursue the crime could ultimately put both of their careers or lives in jeopardy. "Look, even though I know you are embarrassed and angry, I really don't think destroying an officer's career is the answer."

"Baby doll, no one would even know any of us had anything to do with it. It would have been a little messenger passing on a message. Isn't it true this kind of situation is on a need-to-know basis?" Jasmine asked while Monique nodded her head. "Well, her commander needs to know."

CHAPTER 12

Hospital

November 25, 2002

On Monday morning, as usual Lisa was in front of the toilet. The nausea was getting way out of hand to the point she could barely function or concentrate at work. Even her supervisor noticed she was losing a lot of weight.

"Collier, I know you are trying to do your work, but you need to see a doctor. You look horrible," Sgt. Myers said after morning roll call. Lisa sat back in her chair. The room was spinning from the dehydration.

"Ma'am, I'm okay. I just need some juice." She reached for the can of orange juice on the desk. As soon as she took her first sip, she could feel the acid bubbling in her stomach. Sgt. Myers quickly pulled her out of the office into the break room. Lisa collapsed on the couch.

"Airman Collier, you are too sick to be here today. I'll tell you what, how about you call the father and have him come pick you up and take you to the ER?"

Lisa sat up slowly. "I can't."

"Why not? He doesn't have a car?" She sat next to Lisa, rubbing her back.

"He's not in our life," she continued, wiping each tear that fell to her cheek.

Sgt. Myers sat quietly for a moment. "You know I have to ask, right?"

Lisa nodded. Unfortunately, nothing in the military was a secret. She blew out a long air of frustration and began to tell her long, depressing story of the man who once claimed he loved her. Lisa held back her tears as best she could. She convinced herself she cried enough for him.

"He doesn't know about the baby, and I have no way of telling him."

"I'm sorry to hear that, Collier. If you need me to take you, I will."

"Take her where?" Brian interrupted, bursting through the door.

"Hey, Roberts, could you do me a huge favor and I promise I'll go to the supply meeting for you?" she begged.

"Oh, no, I'm fine. It's okay." Lisa sprung to her feet.

"No, you aren't," Sgt. Myers snapped and then turned her attention back to Brian. "I need you to take my airman to the hospital. She is getting worse. I'm going to call my husband and have him put her on the schedule to see the doctor right away."

Brian agreed, and both were on their way to the clinic. Lisa wasn't too thrilled with the idea of Brian being with her, but she was in no condition to argue with anyone. Once they arrived at the clinic, she was taken to the back room for observation. The doctor checked all of her vitals while Brian sat patiently beside her.

"All right, Airman Collier, I'm going to prescribe some medication to help with the nausea. I need you and the father to take it easy with this baby. It looks to me your stress level is high. I think it might be best to put you on half days for the next couple of weeks, and then if we need to, I'll put you on full quarters, or if you get better you can return to full duty. As of right now, you've already lost twenty-one pounds."

"Whoa," Brian blurted.

She gave him a dirty look. "I thought that was normal?"

"Weight loss is normal, but the last time you were here you weighed 145, that was a little over three weeks ago. You are now 124. That's not good. Just take it easy." Major Harris smiled at the young couple. "Okay, Dad, do you have any questions?"

"Yeah, actually, I'm a little concerned because she got into a really bad fight this past Friday," he said. Before she could protest the idea of Brian being the father or the fact he told the doctor she was fighting, she quickly ran over to the sink.

"Okay, the fight may be the reason for some of the problems. Did you see what happened?" Major Harris asked Brian.

"Yeah, I think she was kicked in the stomach a couple of times."

Major Harris shook his head in disbelief. "Keep an eye on her. The baby looks good, but if she starts bleeding or her temperature exceeds normal, it may be early sign of miscarriage."

"Yeah, we definitely don't want that." Brian shook the doctor's hand.

Once the examination was over, Brian took all the paperwork Major Harris gave him and then escorted Lisa to the pharmacy department downstairs.

"Why did you let my doctor think you were the father?" Lisa asked.

"Why is that so bad?"

"You're not the father."

"Look, I'm trying to be a friend. I want you to get through this pregnancy as comfortable as possible. I saw my sister go through her pregnancy alone, and she was miserable." He put his hands on her stomach. She brushed his hand away.

Once she received her medicine, they made their way back to her dorm. In one gulp she swallowed the horse pill, nearly gagging. He sat in the chair across from her while she flopped on her bed, unstrapping her boots. Neither said a word. She fell back and closed her eyes, trying to avoid getting sick again.

"So where is the father?" he asked.

"Wow, you didn't waste any time, did you?" She turned her head to look in his direction.

"Just curious." He shrugged.

"If you really want to know, he's deployed." She sat up and adjusted the pillows so she could get a better view of Brian. "He doesn't know I'm pregnant. By the time I found out, he was already on his way to the desert. We broke up way before I had a chance to tell him." She threw her hands up. "There you have it. Satisfied?"

He got up and sat next to her on the bed. "That's deep."

She shook her head. "I can't do this alone, man, but I don't have a choice."

"Yes, you do. I'm not going anywhere," he said.

CHAPTER 13

The Plan

November 26, 2002

"Sgt. Myers," screamed Anita as she walked into the warehouse. There was no one in sight. She scanned through the vacant office for any sign of life. Her phone began to vibrate, and she quickly answered.

"Hello friend" Lisa greeted groggily.

"Shouldn't you be at work?" Anita responded while logging onto the computer.

"Unfortunately I'm at home on bed rest because the nausea was getting a bit out of control," she explained.

"What happened?"

"Did you talk to Grant?"

"No? Should I?" Anita queried. Lisa explained everything to her about the party and the fight and then went on to explain Brian taking her to the hospital and the baby being in danger. Anita began to feel a little guilty because she wasn't there to defend her friends.

"So is Brian there with you now?" Anita smiled.

"Nope, he left about twenty minutes ago." Lisa sipped her water while flipping through the channels on the TV.

"Is it safe to say you decided to stop being so mean to him?"

"If you're asking me if we're on speaking terms, then yes." Lisa rolled her eyes.

"Aww, he's taking care of you in your pregnancy and you are still just as evil as you want to be." Anita chuckled.

Lisa thought for a moment and then changed the subject. "How was your weekend with the LT?" She laughed.

"Great. Let's just say we may have gotten out of bed once or twice to eat. I had to definitely show that man I should be his future wife." Her eyes widened. "I found my Mr Right, and I am not letting this one go. I never had a man help me with my bills or buy me nice stuff. It's going to be a nice change for me."

"Well done." Lisa clapped loudly over the phone.

"So, back to Mr. Brian," Anita continued.

"You know what, call me later. I'm going to get something to eat." Lisa closed her phone.

"Hello . . ." Anita looked at her phone and noticed the timer flashing.

Jasmine burst through the door, startling Anita. "Nita, Nita," she called out, giving her a hug.

"Don't Nita me, what's this I hear about you fighting?" Anita raised both hands.

"Oh, yeah that." She scratched her head.

"Do I need to pay this woman a visit?" She cracked her knuckles, indicating she was ready for war.

"No, don't worry me, and Monique took care of it on Sunday while the boys were at foot ball practice." Jasmine grinned.

"Care to elaborate?" Anita asked with both eyebrows raised. "Hold up, how did you and Monique get so close?"

"Don't worry about that. Just know I did a little research over the weekend. Come to find out little Ms. Natalie is an officer in the Logistics Readiness Squadron." Jasmine grinned. "So we sat outside of Deon's house for almost four hours waiting for them to leave."

"Why?" Anita asked puzzled.

Jasmine continued. "We found their entire homemade DVD collection. You would not believe some of the video footage they have. They have movies of girls all over this base. I found eight videos of Ms. Natalie in all types of compromising positions with Mr. Deon and in about, oh, I say five more weeks, these videos will be delivered to her commander," Jasmine said with satisfaction.

"Who's Natalie?" Anita asked, frustrated. "And why in five weeks?"

"She's getting promoted. I think these videos will be my promotion gift." Jasmine gave an evil laugh.

"Okay, so then what's next, after you ruin her career? How is this going to help you take Deon down?" she asked.

"My problem isn't with Deon. It's with her. I'm trying to make a point. She had no right to disrespect me at that party. He is a man; he'll get his. But her, she is going to pay now." Jasmine showed her the DVDs in her book bag.

"I can't believe you did that," laughed Anita

"What?"

"You break in their house, steal all of their DVDs, and now you are going to destroy this officer." Anita couldn't believe it made perfect sense. "Sounds logical to me."

"Oh, did I mention I'm going out with Deon this weekend? He's taking me to the movies to apologize for the fight."

"You need to be teaching that dog a lesson." Anita sucked her teeth.

"Oh, trust me, he will. I just haven't figured out how to get him. How do you go after a man who has no morals and doesn't care about anything? Not rules, regulations, or anything," Jasmine thought out loud.

"Surprise me. My man is waiting outside for me so we can go to lunch." Anita pointed to the door.

She walked outside and then scanned the parking lot for Brandon's car. He would flash his light, indicating where he was parked, and she would nonchalantly slip in his car. Anita enjoyed spending a lot of time with Brandon, but she hated the idea of not being able to be seen in public. If they went anywhere, it was always late at night or at his house. They could never be seen at squadron functions holding hands or kissing. It was a very strict relationship that Anita had to learn to cope with. She stopped sleeping in her dorm room and began staying at his apartment. When he came to visit her, he would wear a hat and sunglasses, sometimes even taking it to the extreme and wearing a scarf around his mouth. As bad as things seemed, she knew every relationship paid a price. Some men cheated on their women, and others were broke without a job. Neither one of those factors applied to Brandon. They had already been dating for five magical weeks, and he was more than she could ever imagine. He took her to all the restaurants, shopping sprees until her legs were weak, and romantic getaways to Atlantic City, the Poconos, and New York. Brandon showered her with flowers and candy with anonymous cards at least once a week. *I guess it's not so bad. After, all the officer/enlisted factor is our only dilemma.*

CHAPTER 14

What Lurks in the Dark Eventually Comes to Light

January 21, 2003

*I*t was finally time for Natalie to be promoted to first lieutenant. Her uniform was spotless, and her entire family was there to celebrate, including her secret lover, Deon. The entire squadron stood in the auditorium at attention while Natalie tried to maintain her composure. The projector in the background flashed pictures of her working with the junior enlisted and marching in parades and other squadron events. Jasmine, Lisa, and Anita stood out in the audience while the commander proceeded with the ceremony.

"Attention to orders . . ." the young two-striper quoted from a piece of paper on the podium.

Jasmine couldn't wait for the commander to get back to his office and find the package waiting on his desk. After her five-week investigation, not only did she obtain incriminating video footages of their officer in charge, but she was also able to find love letters she had written to him while deployed to various places, all of which sat waiting to be read and viewed by her boss, who would soon snatch off that silver bar as quickly as he placed it on her shoulders. She couldn't wait to see that cheesy smile dissolve off her face.

Anita eyed her lieutenant while he stood quietly before Natalie, handing the commander her rank to be put on. When the commander was finished, he turned to the squadron to say his final words before dismissing the group. Lisa had been standing next to her, trying to hold her balance. After five weeks of half days, she was finally back to her healthy self, even with her new belly poking through her battle dress blouse. If it wasn't for Brian, she wouldn't have even purchased the maternity uniform. She hated how it looked and preferred to wear his pants.

When the ceremony was over, they all headed back to the office. Anita jumped on her chair and slid to the computer. Lisa and Jasmine sat next to her, going through the stacks of paperwork on the desk.

"So, Lisa, when do we find out what we are having?" Jasmine asked anxiously.

"Not for another two months, but we hear the heartbeat in two weeks." Lisa was excited.

"I'm really surprised at how Brian is taking to this pregnancy. You would've thought he was the father," said Jasmine.

"Well he's not," Lisa retorted.

"Look, Collier, I love you, but you're being unfair. Take a look around. Jerry isn't here; Brian is. You are more blessed than you think. I think it's time you let your guard down and allow this man to help you." Anita begged.

"I see what you are saying, but he can still walk away at any time and there is nothing I can do about it," Lisa continued while filing the scraps of paper in her hand.

"But he hasn't. He has been by your side this entire time. Give him that. You're so scared to trust someone, you keep trying to push him away and he'll do just that," Jasmine agreed.

Lisa's eyes began to swell. Just as Lisa began to speak, Brian walked through the door. She held her lips tight, hoping he wouldn't notice. Jasmine and Anita greeted him with a hug and then walked out so they could be alone.

"Did I miss something, or are they preparing me for bad news?" Brian questioned.

"No, nothing like that." She smiled slightly

"Okay, then what?" He braced for the worst.

"We've been spending a lot of time together, and you've been going to all the appointments." She avoided eye contact. "I need to know are you in this for the long haul or are you just a helping hand?"

Brian burst into laughter. She glared at him.

"Lisa, I care about you. I'm going to be here for you throughout it all. Okay?" He hugged her while she held on to him tightly. "Now let me go before we get in trouble for public display of affection in uniform."

"Oh, shut up." She shoved him playfully.

"I'm sorry, I don't mean to interrupt. I'm looking for Lieutenant Brooks." The young woman entered the office. Lisa jumped away from Brian, hoping the woman hadn't caught them hugging in uniform.

"How are you, ma'am?" He reached for her hand and shook it. Lisa snapped to attention.

"I'm good, and who is this, Airman Roberts?" She turned her attention to the bashful airman standing behind him.

"Hello ma'am, I'm Airman Collier" Lisa smiled sweetly, shaking the woman's hand still standing at the position of attention.

"Oh, sorry, Lisa, this is Lieutenant Brooks's wife. She works in the medical squadron. Her husband works up here with us." He turned back to the woman. "Lieutenant Brooks, this is my wife—oh, sorry." He laughed. "This is my girlfriend, Lisa. She's three months pregnant with my baby," he said proudly.

"Congratulations, Roberts. I knew you would settle down when you found the right one."

"Well, ma'am, let's just say she didn't make life easy for me," he admitted.

"And that's how she's supposed to do it." Lieutenant Brooks winked.

"Ma'am I'm sorry, you are looking for who?" Lisa questioned. She thought long and hard. The name Brooks was all too familiar.

"Lieutenant Brooks," she repeated.

"Lieutenant Brandon Brooks?" Lisa silently prayed. The name was very familiar. It was the same lieutenant Anita had been dating.

"Yes." She gave Lisa and Brian a confused look. "Is he here?"

Lisa quickly shook her head when she realized she was making everyone, including herself, uncomfortable. "Sorry, ma'am, I'm just not here right now. Between this baby and everything going on . . ." She quickly changed her tone when she noticed the odd expression on both individuals' faces.

"It's okay, I've never been pregnant, so I could only imagine."

"Lieutenant Brooks, what I think Airman Collier is trying to say is she's been on half days, so she really doesn't know much of the staff," Brian interrupted.

"Right, my apologies ma'am. This pregnant brain of mine is going to get me in trouble one of these days." She laughed.

Lisa couldn't believe what she was hearing. *Déjà vu.* Thank God in this situation Anita wasn't pregnant. "Brian, uh Airman Roberts . . . I'm sorry, I just remembered I have a lot of work to catch up on, but I'll see you later at home." She waved. "Ma'am, it was nice meeting you."

"Well don't let me hold you back from your duties. It was nice meeting you too," she responded.

She smiled and then proceeded to the warehouse to find Anita. She and Jasmine were in the back on their cell phones when Lisa rushed toward them. The look of horror on Lisa's face was very unsettling. Anita jumped to her feet.

"What's wrong? Is the baby okay?" Anita questioned.

"Brandon's wife is here," she said slowly.

"Brandon, my Brandon?"

Lisa nodded.

"Honey, maybe you misunderstood, because he's not married." Anita smiled.

"Maybe it's a different Brandon," Jasmine interrupted. "Where did you hear this?"

"I didn't hear it from anyone. She walked in while Brian and I were talking, and he introduced her as the wife of Lieutenant Brandon Brooks. They were talking, and then he explained to me that she works in the medical squadron and that she just got back from Kuwait," Lisa rambled.

Anita didn't say a word. She opened her cell phone and dialed Brandon's number. After the second ring, it went to voice mail, so she sent him a text to call her back. After ten minutes, he finally returned her text.

"I'm busy." Anita read the message. "What does he mean he's busy?"

"I'm sure there is an explanation for this," Jasmine comforted. "Collier, what did the woman say exactly?"

"I—" Lisa began to explain.

"It doesn't matter; something is up," Anita interrupted. "I'm going to get to the bottom of this." She closed her phone, walking out of the warehouse.

Brian and Lieutenant Brooks were making their way out of the office. The moment Anita laid her eyes on the stranger; her feet were frozen to the ground. She remembered going through Brandon's wallet and coming across a picture he claimed to be a cousin. It felt like a dream to Anita. The woman in the picture was standing right in front of her, in living color. Only the title the woman claimed was *wife.*

"Collier, is that her?" Anita whispered while still holding on to her chest.

"Yeah." Lisa sighed.

Her breathing became heavy while she replayed all the memories in the house. Nothing seemed out of the ordinary. It was a regular bachelor's pad; there wasn't a single hint another woman had been living there. If she was his wife, where were her clothes or makeup? Anita swore she'd seen enough of that apartment to know another woman did not live there. When she brought herself to move again, she tiptoed into the office, bypassing the woman and Brian. *Think, Anita, think.* Anita paced back and forth in the office and spotted the squadron recall roster. She grabbed the binder, scrolling her finger through all the names and addresses of the unit members. When she came across Brandon's name, she noticed the address listed was different from the apartment. She jotted down all the information and then darted out the door.

"Where are you going?" Lisa screamed before running behind her.

"Nita, wait, we'll come with you." Jasmine followed.

Anita eyed the female lieutenant with a look of pain. Brandon's wife was too busy enjoying the attention she was getting from friends to notice the scorned tornado storming past her. It was obvious from the rock on her finger she was a married woman, but Anita needed something more to prove the betrayal. She ran to a nearby office and grabbed a set of keys off of the table.

"Come on, y'all," she ordered as the three headed to the parking lot.

"Nita, whose keys are those?" Jasmine asked suspiciously.

"Sgt. Myers. Don't worry, we'll be back before her meeting is over," she continued as she hopped into the 2003 Dodge Neon.

"Oh, goodness, we're going to jail!" Lisa cried as she hopped into the backseat.

The three drove for twenty minutes through downtown before pulling up to what looked to be a two-story house, with Brandon's car in the driveway.

"Oh, no . . ." She grabbed her chest. "It's true."

"What do you mean it's true?" questioned Lisa. "You've been here before, right?"

"No, I haven't. He has me shacked up in some apartment in the middle of nowhere while they live in this beautiful house." She looked at the paper to make sure she had written down the correct address. The tears were clouding her vision, but she could see clearly that the numbers matched. Unable to focus, she jumped from the vibration of her phone. She flipped it open to see Brandon's number and answered on the second ring.

"Brandon, I'm in front of your house." She tried to catch herself from screaming into the phone. For a brief moment, everything in her world was crumbling. The man she was falling in love with wasn't hers. "I'm not going to make a scene; I'm not going to be petty. I'm not even going to ask you why you had the audacity to make a fool out of me. Instead I'm going to be the woman I am and just walk away from this nightmare and pretend it never happened."

"Meet me somewhere," he pleaded.

"Are you serious? You parade me around as your little trophy. I find out you're married, and somehow you want me to meet you so you can tell me you're sorry, you didn't mean it? What, Brandon?"

"I can explain. Just let me," he said, making another attempt.

Against her better judgment, she finally agreed to meet him in front of the waterfall where they had first shared their love. Even though she knew her friends supported her, she decided to keep it a secret and go alone. The idea of her going to see a married man for his side of the story was a disaster for continuance. Something inside her wasn't going to let him go. He meant the world to her, and she had finally found someone who was right for her. If anything, his wife would just have to accept it or move on and Anita would be the last one standing.

The all-white Neon slowly pulled into a parking spot close enough for Anita to see Brandon. She took two long breaths as she pushed the door open. Her first thought was to run away as fast as she could. Knowing Brandon, he would stop at nothing to manipulate her to stay with him. Her feet were heavy as she took each step, carefully hoping he wouldn't hear her creeping behind him.

"Run away, Nita," she whispered to herself. "No, he owes you an explanation." She stopped for a moment to look at the tall, handsome deceiver. This was the man she loved, and he broke her heart. There was no way she could forgive him for such a betrayal. "I can't do this," she blurted and then turned to walk away. The bass-tone voice called her name from behind. *Crap, he saw me.* She slowly shifted back to his direction. He was inches away from her, with tears falling down his cheeks.

"I'm sorry I lied to you. We separated after she left for the desert. I was so hurt, I couldn't eat or sleep. Then when I saw you, you changed all that. You made me live life again. And now she wants to work things out." He forced out a couple of whimpers.

"Whose house were you taking me too? And don't tell me one of your deployed friends, because I promise you I will burn it to the ground with you in it!" she demanded.

"No, Nita, I leased that apartment when she left. I needed a place to be on my own and away from all the painful memories," he explained and then grabbed her hand. "Divorcing her is going to be hard. We've been married for almost ten years. She's already entitled to half my retirement." He shook his head, hoping she would feel sympathy for him. "I never wanted you to find out this way. I didn't even know she was in town."

"Explain to me how she is entitled to your retirement."

"In the military, if you've been married for over seven years, you are already entitled to the member's retirement as long as they do their full term and retire. It works out because I'll get half of hers—that's if she does it. I really don't care about all that; it's the house, cars, and other property we have to go through. I'm not ready for all that. As long as she fights this divorce, I'm stuck." He pulled her close to him, hoping she believed his every word. "Nita, I need to know you are going to stay by my side. I can't go through this alone," he lied.

"Of course, whatever, it's me and you." She was happy to hear his explanation.

Brandon had absolutely no intentions of leaving his wife. He was a man of power; money was his weapon of choice. He knew Anita could easily be manipulated. As long as he continued showering her with gifts and romantic getaways, she would always be in his control. A little persuasion and her life was no longer hers.

"Move into my apartment. Whatever you need, I can get it for you. We can do whatever it takes. Just don't leave me. I need to know you'll be there," he continued.

CHAPTER 15

What Comes around Goes Around

January 23, 2003

Lisa couldn't believe she was here, in the hospital with Brian by her side. They were officially a couple. Today they were going to hear the baby's heartbeat. The nurse signaled for them to enter the empty room. As instructed, Lisa took off her BDU blouse and then lifted her shirt. Brian sat quietly in the corner, tapping his legs. Lisa smiled at how nervous he was. He was normally the calm one, but today was different. The nurse walked through the door with a piece of equipment in one hand and a bottle in the other.

"This is going to feel a little cold, but I'm sure you're used to it by now." The nurse smiled while spreading the blue liquid over Lisa's belly. She maneuvered the transducer slightly over her skin for sound waves until she could hear a faint pounding noise.

"Okay, Dad, you'll want to get a recording of this," the nurse said and laughed. His eyes were wide. The beating noise was proof he was going to be a father. The pounding began to sound like waves in the ocean.

"What's that?" Lisa asked, confused.

"Relax, baby was moving." The nurse gently wiped the gel off of Lisa's stomach. Lisa couldn't believe this was her very own baby.

After the appointment, the couple walked side by side into the warehouse. Both were still amazed after hearing their first baby's heartbeat. Neither noticed Natalie storming through the doors with rage in her eyes.

"Brian, we need to talk now," she demanded.

"Good afternoon to you too," he greeted. "What's wrong?"

"Can we talk alone?" she eyed Lisa, who was ready to slap her.

"Let me make sure she's settled first," he said sternly.

"Listen, Airman Collier, I'm truly sorry for the way my friends and I behaved. I swear I didn't even know you were—"

"Airman Collier? Oh, now you want to be professional?" Lisa interrupted. Pregnant or not, she was ready for revenge.

Natalie clenched her teeth. She was too angry to stir up trouble with another enlisted member. Brandon grabbed Lisa's, arm pulling her close to him, and whispered in her ear. The lines on her forehead slowly disappeared as he kissed her forehead.

"Let me see what she wants. I'll catch up with you later."

Lisa smiled and then headed into the office so the two could talk in private. When she entered the office, Jasmine was on her cell phone laughing and carrying on. She hung up the phone when she noticed Lisa.

"How was it?" Jasmine greeted Lisa with a hug.

"It was . . ." Lisa took a deep breath. "Hey, we have very hostile lieutenant outside ranting with Brian. Care to explain?" She crossed her arms, waiting for an explanation. Before Jasmine could say a word, Natalie was hot on her heels, pushing her way into the office. Lisa tried to jump in between them, but Brian pulled her out of the way. Natalie swung for Jasmine, barely missing her jaw. Anita jumped to her feet and pulled Jasmine out of the office by her shirt. Natalie followed behind, grabbing

Jasmine by her neck. Anita tried to break her grip but couldn't. The three fell to the floor.

"Let her go!" Anita screamed, clawing at Natalie's face.

"I'm going to kill you!" Natalie screamed. She pushed Anita's hand away while she pulled at Jasmine's tightly wrapped bun. Jasmine swung her fist as hard as she could, hitting Natalie's cheekbone.

"Not this time!" Jasmine swung her arms as hard as she could. Anita wiggled out of the way and hopped to her feet. The two wrestled while several bystanders made several attempts to separate them.

"Cut it out," Anita yelled while pulling Jasmine off of Natalie.

"I know it was you that sent those tapes to Colonel Jackson," Natalie screamed.

"I didn't do anything; if you weren't living an incriminating lifestyle, you wouldn't have anything to worry about, so don't blame me for your skeletons, Lieutenant," Jasmine yelled back. She quickly calmed herself when she saw her supervisor speed walking toward their direction.

"What is going on here?" Master Sergeant Demarco Lyons hollered. Everyone stood quietly. He examined the two women from head to toe. They were both out of breath, with minor scratches on their neck and faces. "Lieutenant?" he asked with both hands on his hips.

"A discussion got a little out of hand, Sir," Natalie explained in between breaths. Jasmine nodded.

"You in my office now," he demanded. Natalie and Sergeant Lyons disappeared through the gate door. She followed him up the steps into a private office. He slammed the door as hard as he could in frustration.

"What was that about?" he yelled. She lowered her head in shame. "And don't you tell me a little discussion got out of hand. You have no business in this building. If you had a problem, you should've taken it up with Airman Rivera's supervisor."

"I didn't mean for it to get out of control. I was simply asking a question." Natalie never took her eyes off of her boots. She gently touched the swollen marks on her face, reliving the last ten minutes in her head. This wasn't the type of person she was. Somehow she allowed a man to come in and nearly destroy everything she worked so hard for. Unfortunately, there was no one to blame but herself. She squealed in pain.

"Lieutenant Davis, you are not only jeopardizing your promotion but also your career."

"I know that, but she sent my personal videos to Colonel Jackson. I know it was her." She raised her head to look him eye to eye.

"How do you know that, and what kind of videos are we talking about?"

She paused for a moment. "Videos of me and my boyfriend."

"Your boyfriend? Why would Colonel Jackson care about you and your boyfriend?"

"He's enlisted."

"Enlisted? Who?" Sgt. Lyons kept firm eye contact. Natalie knew he wasn't going to back down until she told him the entire truth.

"Sgt. Knight." She kept her head low.

"Doing what?" He glared at her intensely. "You know what? I don't even think I want to know."

It was only a matter of time before she was caught. Engaging in cat fights with junior enlisted was almost psychotic, especially in the professional world. In reality, she was only a few years older than them, but in the military rank was rank.

"Listen—" she began to explain.

"No, you listen! You have lost your mind. Fraternization among officers and enlisted is any kind of personal relationship between each other that violates the customary bounds of acceptable behavior in the air force. You know that. That's a violation of Article 134 in the Uniform Code of Military Justice. You can kiss your promotion good-bye. To top it off, it's an embarrassment to your career. Knight is under your chain of command. There is no way the Colonel is going to let this go without punishment." He rubbed his hands through his graying hair. "I've been in the military for twenty-four years, so officers do not impress me. And if you ever come in here and lay your hand on my airman again, I'll see to it personally you never see the outside of prison walls," he threatened. She nodded.

Anita walked to the parking lot to see Brandon for their usual fifteen-minute visit. She looked around the parking lot, but his car was nowhere in sight. Brandon had never stood her up before; maybe something bad happened. The parking lot was filled with cars, but none of them stood out like his. Bright lights flashed in front of her where she noticed a tan-colored 2003 Toyota Camry. When she noticed Brandon behind the wheel, she slowly eased into the vehicle.

"Wow, this is nice. Where's the beamer?" she asked, rubbing the suede seats. The stereo system was equipped with a CD player and slide-out TV monitor.

He smiled. "My BMW is parked at my shop; this brand new vehicle is for my number-one beauty."

Her eyes widened from shock. She couldn't believe he actually bought her a car. "Are you . . . This is my . . . Oh, my goodness, thank you." She wrapped her arms tightly around his neck.

"Yep, this is your new car." He pulled the keys from the ignition and dangled them in front of her face. "This key is for your car, and this one is for your apartment." He pointed at each key and then placed them in her hands.

"Brandon, I can't afford all this." Her smile faded as she put the keys back into his hands.

"Don't insult me, Nita." He shoved them back to her. "I bought all of this for you, which means I'm responsible for all the bills. You don't have to worry. Do you hear me?" he waited for her response.

"Okay, so you do all this, then what do I have to do in return?" she asked, already knowing the answer.

He smiled at the open offer. "Simple. I take care of you, and you, missy, take care of me."

Anita burst through the warehouse as if she'd just won the lottery. She ran toward Lisa, who'd been placing labels on boxes. Lisa was caught off guard when Anita almost ran into her.

"What's up with you?" Lisa questioned.

"Look." Anita dangled the keys in front of Lisa's face. "He just bought me a brand-new car and asked me to move into his apartment."

"Brandon?" Lisa asked, surprised.

"Yes, Brandon. We talked, and we're going to work it out," she said softly.

Lisa exhaled. "He must love you, girl. You guys have only been together for a short amount of time and already he's putting you on wife-replacement status."

"I know. He's really special to me, but it bugs me with the whole wife situation. He does everything for me." She looked at the keys in her hand. "So are you going to help me move into my new apartment?"

"As much as I can. Who's paying for this stuff anyway?" Lisa questioned.

"Everything is in his name, so he said I could leave at any time if I wanted to and there will be no penalties, you know, with credit and stuff. But he lost his mind. There is no way I'm leaving any of this." She jingled the keys in the air.

"Okay, so when do we move in?"

Anita's smile disappeared when she noticed Lisa swollen belly. "On second thought, why don't you send that strong man of yours to come help me? I will not be held responsible for any mishaps with your pregnancy."

Lisa and Anita walked into building where Deon, Mark, and Brian were standing around laughing and joking with Sgt. Myers.

"Hey, ladies, where you been?" Sgt. Myers questioned, with one eyebrow raised.

"In the back of the warehouse putting some boxes away," said Anita.

"Yep, and bragging about that new car her man bought her." Lisa elbowed Anita, who was grinning from ear to ear.

"Hmmm, that's nice. He must be something special, buying you expensive gifts. I don't know any of the junior enlisted who can afford to buy someone else a car, let alone afford their own payments." She eyed Anita, whose smile turned into a frown.

"Sgt. Myers, I'll put the rest of those boxes up for you." Anita rolled her eyes. She refused to allow Sgt. Myers to criticize a relationship she would never approve of anyway. After all, it wasn't her business. "Collier, I'll catch you later. Good day, gentlemen." She waved while reaching for the cart full of boxes and headed for the warehouse.

Sgt. Myers followed behind, but Anita kept walking.

"Look, Jefferson, I know you think that I'm coming down hard on you, but you need to understand I'm only looking out for your best interest," Sgt. Myers explained.

"Ma'am, no disrespect, but you don't know anything about me or my situation, so I would greatly appreciate if you allowed me to get back to my work." She slowly lifted one of the boxes onto a shelf. "We care a lot about each other, and that's my business."

"Okay, then why is he such a big secret? If he is so special, why do you only meet him in the parking lot? Don't think I haven't noticed you tiptoeing out of here to meet Mystery Man on duty hours. And keep in mind, this is your career." She pointed at her. "Don't let some man come in and do for you what you can do for yourself. In the end, this early it's going to destroy you. I've seen too many young airmen come in here on cloud nine just to fall on their behinds and get hurt. All I'm asking is to be smart about it, okay?"

"Yes ma'am." Anita wasn't trying to sit through an hour-long lecture. Nothing she said registered in her brain as being remotely pertaining to her. Brandon loved her deeply and did everything for her. That was all that mattered.

Why are people in the Air Force so nosy? Sgt. Myers doesn't even know what she's talking about. Why do I have to bring Brandon around strangers just to prove he loves me? She probably wants to meet him hoping she could steal him away from me.

CHAPTER 16

Back to Reality

May 15, 2003

Lisa was only weeks away from her eighth month. Both parents were beyond anxious to welcome their new son into the world. Her belly was round, sticking straight through her maternity battle dress she had dreaded wearing. Since the due date was almost near, Brian was hounding her every minute of every day. He'd call her cell phone multiple times a day to make sure she'd eaten and taken her prenatal vitamins. Mark, Devon, and Deon doubled her stress by adding three extra pair of eyes on her. They would tell Brian if she was working too hard or if she wasn't in her dorm room at a certain time. They were getting on her last nerve. Her hormones were making her irritable, which she took out on Brian every chance she got. There was nothing he could do to remedy her mood swings. He thought distancing himself from her until she had the baby would make her miss him and things would go back to the way they were. This only made things worse with her insecurities.

Jasmine and Deon were still dating. However, he was still determined not to add another Natalie in his life. After the commander caught wind of her with an enlisted member, her promotion was suspended and she was moved to another squadron until further action could be taken. Deon never heard from her. He would see her from time to time, but she never made eye contact. It was said the commander spared her from being dishonorably discharged. Although Jasmine was happy to rid herself of Natalie and focus on her new man, she still wasn't finished yet. Deon still had to pay for his crimes of her embarrassment and endangering her and her friends' lives for five minutes of entertainment.

Anita moved into Brandon's apartment, living the life of luxury of the rich and famous. Brandon paid any and every bill Anita accumulated, and she in return paid him handsomely with sexual favors. There were no boundaries for her because in love there was no such thing. He'd convinced her into having threesomes, performing oral sex, strip teasing, videotaping—anything his wife wouldn't do she was surely gracious enough to do it. He was very thankful for Anita's generosity. She thought she had the perfect life until one night Anita came home late from a party she'd been at with Jasmine. Brandon told her he was staying home with the wife for the weekend to discuss plans about divorce, so Anita figured she would chill out with the girls. When she came home, Brandon was fuming and angry, waiting on the couch for her.

"Do you know what time it is?" he stated angrily while looking at his watch.

"Hey, I thought you weren't coming over this weekend," she said, wondering why he was sitting in the dark. As she reached for the light switch, she noticed Brandon's eyes were bloodshot red and he smelled of alcohol.

"Oh, okay, so when I'm gone trying to handle business for our future, you want to hang out all hours of the night with your friends." He stood up and walked toward her.

"Now you know it's not even like that. I was out with Jasmine having a little girl time. Come on now." She laughed it off.

"Forget this. I'm going back to my house. I thought we could spend the evening together, but you want to be out with other men. Is that how it is? You don't want a good man. You want these fools out here with no life and no money while I'm home paying for the car you're driving and the house your living in rent-free. I guess I'm the fool," he hollered while walking out the door.

"Brandon!" she called after him, but it was too late. *I can't believe this.*

Anita tried to catch him before he jumped into his car. She attempted grabbed the driver-side handle. Brandon pressed firmly on the gas pedal, causing her to jump backward to avoid being hit.

"Brandon!" she screamed again.

When she noticed the neighbors flicking on their lights and opening their doors, she ran into the house in search of her cell phone. She tried to call him but the rings went straight to voice mail. After almost two hours, he finally picked up.

"Baby, I'm sorry," she cried.

"*Baby*? Who is this?" a strange woman asked.

Anita couldn't bring herself to say a word. *Oh, no. I hope that wasn't his wife. What if I got him into trouble?*

"Look, I don't know who you are, but this is his girlfriend, Tiffany, and I don't appreciate you calling this late at night. As a matter of fact, I would appreciate it if you didn't call him at all," Tiffany continued and then hung up the phone.

Anita couldn't believe her ears. It was bad enough she had to share him with his wife; it was even worse when she had to share him with other women. She closed her phone, contemplating what she was going to do. There was no way she was going to allow another woman to intrude in the happy home she was building. She called back, but it went straight to voice mail.

It was after midnight when Anita was awakened by a man's hand. She jumped, fearing an intruder, but felt relieved when she saw Brandon.

"You scared me." She sprung up.

"I'm sorry. Look, I know I overreacted. I can do that at times. It's me—I'm so used to order and being in control," he admitted.

"I called your phone." She tried to hold back her tears.

He didn't say a word; he was secretly praying the confrontation between the two women was just a dream. Tiffany had lectured him for almost an hour about other women calling his phone. He simply shut her up with flowers and a trip to Atlantic City. Now it was time to put the wheels in motion with Anita. What was it going to take for her to let it go and get him off the hook?

"Not only do I have to worry about your wife, but now you have another girlfriend," she continued but refused to look him in the eye.

"No, she wants to be my girlfriend. She must've answered my phone when I was in the bathroom or something. There is no way I would allow another woman to disrespect you like that." He gave her his best "I'm sorry" look, hoping she would accept his apology.

"You must think I'm a fool," Anita continued.

"Babe, I promise, you are the only woman I want. Don't you think if I didn't care about you I would be with my wife right now, pretending to be the family man she wants me to be?" He raised his voice a little. "No, I'm with you. Why? Because I love you and you are the one I want to be with."

"Brandon, I appreciate everything you do for me, but if this happens again, I'm leaving you for good." She leaned forward to kiss him on the cheek. "I don't want to fight with you."

As much as she didn't want to be the fool, love was blind and so was she. All she could do was forgive the cheater in front of her. Maybe with a little bit more time and a little bit more patience, he would come to realize she was the right woman for him.

"Baby, when you get off work, I want to show you something." Brandon smiled as he pulled up to the warehouse.

"I can't wait." She kissed him on his lips before departing the car.

Sgt. Myers watched from the warehouse door, shaking her head. Anita glared at her; she wasn't in the mood for a lecture.

"Airman Jefferson, can I speak to you for a moment?" Sgt. Myers asked sternly.

"No, ma'am, I have a lot of work to catch up on," Anita mumbled, brushing past her.

Anita stormed into the office while Sgt. Myers strolled behind her. Lisa was on the computer when the two came bursting into the room, arguing.

"What's going on?" Lisa questioned.

"Did you know about this?" Sgt. Myers questioned Lisa. Anita sucked her teeth.

"About . . ." Lisa was totally oblivious to the entire conversation.

"Lieutenant Brooks," she responded, and then she directed her attention toward Anita. "Anita, you already know—" Sgt. Myers began.

"Ma'am, he was just being nice. He saw me walking from the dorm and gave me a ride," Anita replied, disinterested in the conversation.

"Jefferson, do you really think I'm that stupid?" Sgt. Myers continued. "I know about your so-called relationship you got going on, and let me tell you, you're playing with fire."

Anita looked at her, speechless. There was nothing she could say without getting herself into trouble or Brandon, for that matter. She bit her tongue, trying to avoid saying anything that would cause the argument to get out of hand.

"Sgt. Myers, I am very aware of fraternization. I'm not going to jeopardize the career of a lieutenant."

"Well how about adultery? He could get a year in prison for this if he's charged and convicted, either that or dishonorable discharge." Sgt Myers continued, "You young little airmen come up in here swearing you know every rule and detail when the truth is you don't know anything about the military. You make stupid decisions and then walk around here dumbfounded because you can't figure out where you went wrong. He is a married man. Not only were you being selfish, but you didn't think about how his wife would feel knowing you were trying to destroy her marriage."

"His marriage was over a long time ago. I had nothing to do with that." She crossed her arms in frustration. "Lisa, haven't you noticed that everything involving an officer ends with jail time? Is it just me or does this sound a bit redundant?" She waited for Lisa's response.

"Well actually . . ." Lisa began, but Sgt. Myers cut her off.

"Stay out of this, Airman Collier." The look on Sgt. Myers's face could have killed. "May I remind you that I am a noncommissioned officer, so you will respect me like one. I'm not here to get you in trouble . . . yet! But I will if you continue this charade with him."

Anita turned her attention back to her supervisor, ready to fight words with words. "First off, no disrespect, Sgt. Myers, but he is leaving his wife. It's because of this whole officer marriage thing he has to go through a lot in which he isn't ready, so I'm going to stand by him until they settle everything and get their divorce," Anita snapped.

Sgt. Myers laughed at the naive child. "Did he tell you that? Did he tell you he loved you and that he couldn't live without you? I bet he was saying this while you two were having sex, huh?"

Anita didn't bother to answer.

Sgt. Myers sighed. "Anita, you weren't the first he's done this to, and you won't be the last."

"How do you know?" Lisa interrupted.

"Come on, Collier, I know you guys are young, but you can't be this naive to men in power." Sgt. Myers took a deep breath and then continued. "These men around here are about making money and taking charge. They control these little hothead females, and all it takes is a flash of a smile and a hundred-dollar bill and then you all fall to pieces." She walked over to her desk and sat down. "Jefferson, I can almost bet he's paying for the apartment you are trying to hide, which I kept quiet about. The car you are driving, the cell phone you are using, and the clothes you are wearing all came from his bank account."

"So what, now it's a crime for a good man to take care of his woman?" Anita spat.

"Yes, because you are not his woman! When he spends that kind of money on you, it means that every time he quotes sleeps around on you or orders you around, it makes it that much harder for you to leave. He showed his Prince Charming side, spoiled you rotten, and then took over your life as if he was your creator." She laughed.

"You sound jealous," responded Anita.

"Jealous? Let me tell you something. My husband may not be buying me expensive gifts and showering me with nonsense, but at least I know where he lays his head at night. And I'm number one. I've met his parents. I got the credit cards, house keys, the ring, and benefits. Oh, yeah, and at least I can go wherever I please all hours of the day with my husband because, like I said, I have the covenant!" Sgt. Myers glared at Anita. "I'm not going to sit up here and try to convince you I've been with the most faithful man in the world, but at least I've always been the lead woman in charge."

Jasmine walked in and saw Anita fuming with her arms crossed. Judging from the vibe in the room, she could tell something was wrong.

"What's going on?" she asked, puzzled.

CHAPTER 17

Trouble in Paradise

June 23, 2003

"*J*asmine, I have been trying to call Brian all night. He texted me and said he had stuff to take care of, but it's almost nine. Where is he? I'm worried about Nita, I'm eight months pregnant, and my boyfriend is out with who knows who." Lisa began to panic while pacing back and forth in her room.

"Lisa, you need to calm down. I'm sure he's probably out with Deon terrorizing the streets," Jasmine comforted while holding the receiver on her shoulder.

Lisa took a deep breath into the phone. "Jasmine, he's been hanging out a lot lately. I could deliver anytime."

"Let's hope not. What he say about you two getting an apartment together?" Jasmine changed the subject.

"Unfortunately, I can't move into base housing until the baby is born, so I'm stuck in the dorms." Lisa sounded disappointed.

"What about off base?"

"I put my name on the list to move out, went to the briefings, but I'm not sure I can even afford that. At least in base housing I don't have to put any money down. The civilians up there said I can write a letter requesting to move out early since I'm already in the third trimester and the baby is healthy," Lisa explained.

"I hope you get it."

"Me too." Lisa looked at her phone to see Brian was on the other line. "Hey, girl, hold on." She clicked over. "Hello?"

"Baby, I'm staying at Deon's tonight. So I'll call you later, okay?" Brian rushed.

"Huh, what's going on? This is the fourth night in a row," Lisa whined.

"Hey, I got to go—De needs to show me something." *Click*

"Huh, hello?"

"Yeah, girl?" Jasmine responded. "What's wrong?"

"That was Brian. He practically rushed me off the phone to tell me he was staying at Deon's. Have you talked to him?"

"Nope. He said he had some business to take care of."

"I think we are going to pay them a little visit tonight." Lisa was steaming mad.

"Lisa, let's not start with the insecurities. Brian is a good man. He's been there. Why all of a sudden would he start cheating?"

"I don't care. He's been acting funny."

"If you push that man with false pretenses, he's going to start cheating," Jasmine warned.

"Come get me in ten minutes." Lisa closed her phone and went to change out of her BDUs.

When they approached Deon's house, Brian's car was nowhere in sight. Lisa could feel a fire burning inside her. Her anxiety was making her shake. *Where is he?* She pulled out her cell to call him, but it went straight to voice mail.

"Voice mail," Lisa said while slamming the phone down.

Jasmine took a deep breath. "Okay, now what?"

"Do you think Deon would know where he is at?" she asked.

"Even if he did, he wouldn't tell me." Jasmine was confused at the two lovebirds who were practically ready to jump off the bridge and get married. "Where did all of this come from? One moment he's calling you every twenty minutes and now he's not coming home and cutting off his cell phone."

"Ever since I got into the last month, he's been acting weird. At first he tried to say I changed, but it's him."

Lisa thought for a moment. She only had one choice, and that was to wait until the morning time when she knew his phone would be turned back on. Jasmine started the car and headed back to the dormitory. Neither said a word. Jasmine knew Lisa was angry. She only wished she could help her friend. For the rest of the evening, Lisa couldn't sleep. She tossed and turned in her bed, waiting for him to call.

The sun peaked through the curtains, shining a strip of light onto Lisa's face. Her eyes fluttered opened. After completing her morning regimen, she headed off for work. Thoughts of Brian's late nights began to bother her. As much as she wanted to, she wasn't ready for any confrontations. Brian went from calling four or five times a day to one quick five-minute call.

Lisa and Jasmine were working in the warehouse when her phone began to vibrate. She flipped it open to see Brian's number.

"Now he's calling." Lisa rolled her eyes. She hit the ignore button and then closed her phone. "I'm going to beat him at his own game."

"How long are you going to ignore him? You know that baby could come any day now, and you are in no position to play hide and seek."

Lisa ignored her and continued walking to work. Brian continued to call, but Lisa refused to answer the phone. They were almost done with their work when they headed back to the office. Jasmine grabbed Lisa's arm and pointed in the direction Brian was walking. The wrinkle between his eyebrows told them he was not in a good mood. The girls turned back into the large storage area.

"I need to hide, Jasmine," she panicked.

"Calm down. We'll sit out here and wait until he leaves."

Lisa's phone vibrated over and over again. She didn't have to look at it to tell it was Brian. They ran to the very end of the warehouse where all the tires were stored. Both slipped into one of the empty storage spaces.

"I don't think he'll come back here. He knows you aren't allowed back here anyway," said Jasmine. "So what's the plan?"

"I'm not sure what my plan is. All I know is I can't face him right now." She looked and saw that Brian had left her four messages and three text messages. "I'm not reading them, and I'm not going to hear what he has to say. This is some bull. I've been a good woman to him, and he's out every night turning off his phone."

"Okay, so avoiding him is the answer? Lisa, you are so close to your due date. What are you going to do, confront him when you're in labor?" Jasmine questioned.

"Hey, at least I know I'll be yelling louder than him," she responded. "Tonight I'm going to your house. I know he'll be at the dorms waiting for me. Jasmine, you have to promise not to tell Deon where I'm at."

"Okay, I wont," Jasmine agreed.

CHAPTER 18

A New Beginning

July 16, 2003

Lisa's due date was almost around the corner. She'd been dodging Brian for almost two weeks. Whenever he would stop by the office, she would hide in the warehouse or upstairs. She had lookouts telling her if he was coming or going. He'd call her all hours of the day, but she was determined not to answer. The squadron picnic was coming up, and Sgt. Myers volunteered her and Anita to help. They had to plan the event, sell tickets, and worst of all, be there from beginning to end. She knew she was going to eventually have to face him. But what would she say? He'd been calling so much she made it a point to leave her phone home. She even started camping on Jasmine's couch. His home was her dorm, so there was no place else to go. She loved Anita, but she refused to stay around all of that marriage drama. It would only be a matter of time before Brandon's wife caught wind of his affair and shot up that little apartment.

"Brian just won't give up. As big as I am, I can't be running around every time I see him," Lisa said while totaling the cost of the picnic at her desk.

"What are you trying to prove again, may I ask, by ignoring this man?" Anita questioned while finishing the flyer for the event that was only a day away.

"Anita, don't start. I don't know what I'm trying to do. At this point I'm so out of it. I'm just not in the mood for any confrontations."

"Brian cares for you. I know he does. No man would step up and father a child he had nothing to do with," Anita advised.

"Anita, I know that. But he lied to me, and I can't trust him. So for once, just be on my side and trust that I'm going to handle this." Lisa was becoming frustrated.

Anita stood up and then gave Lisa a hug. "I know it's hard on you since Jerry up and disappeared. Monique told me that Gerard still talks to him."

"Wow, which makes me feel better."

"He told him about the baby," Anita continued.

"What?" She stood up and then felt around for her phone. "I don't have my phone. Let me see yours," Lisa demanded.

Anita instantly grabbed her cell and then dialed Monique's number. The moment Monique answered; Lisa was already running her mouth about Jerry. She couldn't believe her best friend wouldn't tell her that she'd been keeping contact with him. The two were shouting back and forth.

"I can't believe you've been talking to Jerry this entire time knowing that I was suffering being pregnant alone. I never got the chance to talk to him, tell him how much I'm hurting right now, and all along my own best friend knew where he was," she screamed.

"Okay, I know that your hormones are really messing with your brain because you wouldn't dare think to raise your voice at me. First off, I don't talk to Jerry. Gerard does. They're friends. What am I supposed to do, tell him to cut him off?"

"Why didn't you tell me that? Then you tell him that I'm pregnant and don't even bother to give me a heads-up—or anything, for that matter."

Lisa threw the cell phone back at Anita and walked into the warehouse. Anita stayed on the phone while following behind Lisa.

"Anita, leave me alone," Lisa cried.

"Lisa, she says that Gerard told him after he found out that Brian was in the picture. Monique didn't tell Jerry anything. When Gerard started hearing rumors about your pregnancy, he asked Monique, so she told him the truth. She wanted Jerry to know that he left a wonderful woman who was carrying his child and that another man is doing the job he should've been doing," Anita repeated while listening to Monique's side of the story. "Gerard said that Jerry wants to be there, but Monique wouldn't give him your number because she didn't want to destroy everything you and Brian had. She loves Brian."

Lisa grabbed the phone from out of Anita's hand. "I'm sorry, girl. I didn't mean to yell at you. It's just this pregnancy is really getting to me, and Brian is messing around on me. I just wish I wasn't pregnant. I wish I never met either one of them."

Anita's heart sank. "Collier, you don't mean that." She sat next to Lisa. Monique continued what she was saying before they hung up.

"Nita, why do I feel like this is Ashley all over again?"

"It isn't. You are just emotional, and you think pushing everybody out of your life is going to make things better. It's only going to make things worse."

July 28, 2002

It was the annual LRS Picnic, and the entire squadron came out to baseball field directly across from the warehouse to enjoy the festivities. Anita and Lisa had been setting up decorations when Brian, Deon, Brandon, and Devon walked to the baseball field across the street from the warehouse. Lisa felt her heart drop into her stomach when she saw Brian walking toward her.

"Anita, hide me," she screeched.

"No, face him." Anita pulled her arm toward Brian.

He had a frown on his face, and judging from his body language, he wasn't too happy with the hide-and-seek games she'd been playing.

"Care to explain to why you've been hiding?" His voice was stern.

"Care to explain to me why you lied to me? Care to explain you not coming home at night? Or how about turning off your phone?" She tried to match her attitude with his.

"What late nights? I told you I was with Deon," he explained. "Is that what this is about?"

"You are going to sit here and lie to me to my face. That night you called and said you'd be at Deon's house and then hung up with no further explanation. I went over there. I didn't see your car. As a matter of fact, I called your phone several times that night, and for some odd reason, it went to voice mail." She sucked her teeth. "You must think I'm stupid enough to believe your lies, but I come from a whole line of dogs, so I know the game. You got one chance, and if you lie to me, then you've lost this battle and you can walk away from me and never have to worry about this child you agreed to step up and be a father to." She cleared her throat and crossed her arms. "Now have you been messing around on me?"

Her eyes were fixed on his, waiting for his reaction. She knew the last thing she wanted to do was leave him, but she'd rather be alone then be a fool for another man. The baby in her belly was a reminder of a man she went against her gut feeling for and decided to give a chance.

"Okay, since you want to be a little private investigator and follow me around, well then yes. Are you happy? You too busy snapping on me, and all I ever done was be there for you. I stepped up and didn't know anything about you. I took the abuse from you long enough. And when another woman showed me that she appreciated all the little things I did for her, like call her and tell her I was thinking about her or send her flowers, that made me feel good. I guess I should've known expecting any kind of appreciation from you wasn't happening. So yes, she was there for me. Do I like her? Yes, I do. Does she make me happy? Yes, she does. Do I want to be with her?" He paused and then noticed she was becoming upset. "Lisa, I love you, but I can't keep taking this madness from you anymore. I'm out." He shook his head and then walked away.

She felt like falling to the floor. Her knees were weak from his words. *Did he really just leave me for someone else?* Anita had been listening the entire time. She ran to Lisa's side once Brian was no longer in sight. The wind had been knocked out of her chest. *Please let this be a dream. It's Jerry all over again.* Her pride kept her from stopping him. The entire scene flashed back to the moment Jerry walked away from her. She was a woman scorned; maybe she took it out on Brian. Maybe he deserved another woman. Obviously she wasn't being fair to him. This wasn't his child. He deserved his own baby. Again she was alone. Anita comforted her, but her world nearly came to a halt when she noticed Brandon and his wife hugging, laughing, and enjoying life together. As much as she didn't want to admit it, they looked like a happily married couple. He'd been in the same vicinity as Anita for almost two hours and never once acknowledged her with so much as a wink. She'd never been around them when they were together. He was a proud man next to his trophy wife. She envisioned herself on his arm, laughing with friends, but knew in the military that was far from reality.

"I can't believe this." Anita sighed at the beautiful couple. "It never hit me until I actually saw them together." She shook her head. "I hate to admit it, Collier, but Sgt. Myers was right." She laughed at herself for being naïve.

"Nita, my water broke." Anita turned to see her friend on the floor grabbing her stomach. Her pants were soaked with amniotic fluid.

"Oh, my goodness." Anita panicked. She screamed for help. The entire picnic came to a standstill. People were coming from every angle to Lisa's aid. She grabbed the nearest person she could and held on tightly to his hand. The poor man moaned in pain at her grip. Lisa was breathing heavily, and she could barely concentrate.

"Okay, Collier, you need to calm down and focus on your breathing," the sergeant said, holding on to her hand. He slipped underneath her while she lay in between his legs. He demonstrated breathing techniques while she held on tight through each contraction, but the pain was too much. The contractions were getting closer.

"Oh, it hurts," she screamed. The sergeant continued coaching her until she was able to keep a steady breathing pace.

Brian wasn't too far away when he noticed the crowd. After hearing a woman scream, he could tell Lisa was in labor. He ran to her side, fighting through the crowd. "Baby, calm down. I'm here, okay?" he said, squatting down in front of her. Lisa was very happy to see him in front of her.

"Is he the father?" asked the sergeant. She looked up at him, unable to answer.

"Yeah, I'm the father," he interrupted, smiling at Lisa. She returned the smile and then pulled him closer.

"Brian, I'm so sorry . . . I know I messed up. Just give me . . . whew . . . a chance and I . . . owwwwww . . . I promise I'll get better," she said in between deep breaths.

"Don't worry about it, just say we're even." He imitated the sergeant's breathing so that Lisa would continue.

"Collier, I've called the police. They are sending an ambulance right away," Sgt. Myers interrupted.

"Oh, no, I can't wait. We have to go now. I feel the baby coming." Lisa screamed while digging her fingers into Brian's arms. Brian cringed at the pain.

Three guys from the vehicle shop ran for the nearest government vehicle. The pickup pulled up next to the field while Brian and Deon lifted Lisa off of the ground into the truck.

"Are you guy's crazy? You are going to put me in the back of a pickup truck like some hillbilly?" she yelled.

"You got a better idea?" Deon responded and then pulled her into the vehicle against her wishes. Anita and Jasmine jumped in the back with Lisa.

The vehicle guys put the car in gear and then sped off. They were going sixty in a twenty-five, radioing security forces to catch up and escort them through town, in case the police tried to stop them. They had to drive to the civilian hospital since the facility on base didn't have a maternity ward.

"Brian, this is illegal. We are going to jail," Lisa cried.

"Don't you worry about that. Just worry about having my son, you hear me?" He rubbed her back.

She could see all the attention the unauthorized vehicle was getting from the pregnant women in the back to the police cars flashing lights. She secretly prayed they wouldn't get in trouble with the wing commander. When they reached the hospital, Lisa was dragged through the emergency entrance. She was hunched over, unable to walk. The doctors and nurses took immediate action. Brian followed while they wheeled her upstairs to the maternity area. The pressure from the baby made her feel lightheaded. After twenty minutes, she could feel the doctors cutting her uniform. The pain was getting worse. Brian sat back and watched the action taking place.

"Ms. Collier, you are more than six centimeters, so we won't be able to give you an epidural. In the meantime we'll try to give you some pain medication through your IV," the nurse said while pushing a needle into her vein.

"Oh, goodness," she cringed. Brian stood next to her and held her hand.

"Don't worry, babe, you can do this. You're strong enough," Brian encouraged.

"Thanks." She smiled. He leaned over to kiss her forehead, but she jerked in pain. "Nurse, he's coming out. I can feel him in between my legs." She screamed.

The nurse looked under the blanket and noticed the crown of the head. Lisa screamed in pain. Doctors rushed by her side, breaking apart the bed. Brian felt nauseous at all the blood. After three pushes, their son was out. Brian Jr. weighed nine pounds and three ounces. He was twenty-one inches long. They cleaned him up then placed him on Lisa, who was in awe of her new baby boy.

"Wow, I can't believe he's so beautiful," Lisa said, looking around for Brian. "Nurse, where's Brian?"

The nurse laughed, pointing to the floor where had Brian passed out.

"Is he okay?" she panicked.

"Yeah, he'll be fine," said the nurse.

When Brian came to, Lisa was already medicated and fast asleep. He noticed something moving in the tiny bed next to her. The pain in his head reminded him of the fall, but he slowly made his way to his son. The tiny baby was wide awake, staring at the man he would call father. In quick swoop, Brian picked him up, admiring the life his love brought into the world. It didn't matter this child wasn't his blood. All the fighting and abuse Lisa put him through were all worth the feeling of being a father. His son shared his first and last name. He watched her while she slept. She was so beautiful. His phone rang, interrupting the moment

"Hello," he answered while staring at his beautiful queen.

"Hey, baby, where you at? I was thinking we could catch a late movie tonight," the excited young woman said.

"That won't be a good idea," he said, still staring at his newborn son in admiration.

"You didn't return my text. Everything okay?" the girl asked, concerned.

"Yeah, everything is cool. Hey, I need to call you back. I'm with my son right now," he replied.

"What?" was the last word he heard before closing his phone. He wanted to start his family off right, and that meant cutting off any and all other females.

The nurse walked in and handed Brian a paper. "Okay, Dad, fill this out and sign it," she said, handing him a pen.

"What is this?" he eyed the paper suspiciously.

She smiled. "It's for Brian Junior's birth certificate." He returned a smile and grabbed the application. It was official; even on paper, Brian Jr. was his. Now it was time to make Lisa his on paper.

July 31, 2002

After spending three days in the hospital, Lisa, Brian, and Junior arrived to their new home in base housing. Brian was able to set up so all of Lisa's and his things were moved into the apartment. Jasmine and Anita chipped in their support and purchased new furniture for the happy couple's home. It was a small two bedroom, but to Brian and Lisa, it was a start of a new beginning. Lisa walked in and couldn't believe how beautiful the new house was. It was one floor located at the end of the set of row homes. The girls really brought the house style. She spun around; arms wide open at her new place. When she turned to look at Brian, he was on one knee with a two-carat diamond ring in his hand. Jasmine and Anita were smiling from ear to ear.

"Oh, my goodness, is this for real?" Lisa was ready to cry.

"Lisa, I know that we haven't been the best boyfriend and girlfriend, but after giving me a son, I know that this is my family and I'm going to fight for you two. I want you in my life forever. In order for us to start a family, we need to do this right, so will you marry me?"

She slowly walked toward him. "Brian, are you serious?" She smiled and then nodded her head. "Of course I'll marry you!"

He jumped up and then grabbed her. She slid on her new diamond ring. It was white gold with three diamonds, past, present, and future.

Anita eyed her phone as Brandon's name appeared on the display screen. The flashback of him with his wife hurt deep to her soul. Watching the birth of Junior and seeing Brian propose made her see what she truly wanted. Brandon was never going to give her that. She put her phone away and then walked toward Jasmine, who was holding Junior, admiring his tiny features.

"Hey, girl, I need a favor," she said.

"What's up?" Jasmine didn't take her eyes off of the baby.

"I'm going to move my stuff out of Brandon's apartment. Do you think you or your roommate would mind a third wheel?"

"Of course, you know you're always welcome to stay with us. What made you come to your senses?"

"My nephew made me realize that I want a family, and Brandon is not going to give it to me." She let out a slight laugh.

"Okay and do you really think Brandon is going to just up and let you leave like that?" She raised her eyebrow.

"No, this is why I'm going to move out while he's at work." She winked.

August 1, 2002

Anita stepped into the apartment that was the basis all of the pain and lies she held. How was she going to tell her family she let a man fool her into believing he was the one for her? She eyed all the pictures of them on the wall. None of them were worth keeping. She bit her pride and told Sgt. Myers the truth; in return, she let her take a "sick" day to move out. Her clothes were neatly packed into Jasmine's car. Before leaving, she left all her keys, phone, and a letter on the dining room table.

It read:

Dear my love,

I know you might be a little confused at my choice to leave, but let's face it. I saw you and your wife at the picnic. You spent the last five months telling me things weren't working out and that you would leave her when the time was right. I'll admit I was naive to believe you, but my eyes are open now. You can't keep me on display. I'm not your trophy to brag about to your phony friends. I'm returning your keys and your phone. I'm keeping all the clothes and jewelry. I think after all the humiliation you put me through; I deserve something out of this. You can keep the pictures as a reminder of the beauty who would do anything for you out of love. You say I took you for granted, but the truth is, I wasn't your woman. I was your prostitute, at your beck and call. Yes, you got the last laugh, but I won't let you control me anymore. I'm taking over. I bought my own phone, I'm living in my own house, and all this with no help from you. Don't worry, I won't speak about your indiscretion. It won't do me any good for your wife to know that I was your mistress. So I'm leaving you now. There is no bad blood on my part, so when you see me in the streets, I'll smile and wave, but it will never be the way it was. I'm sure you'll find someone else to replace me. You'll spoil her and make her feel like an in-house queen, but be careful because hell hath no fury on a woman scorned.

Love Always,
Anita Jefferson

CHAPTER 19

Old Skeletons

August 6, 2003

onique was sad she missed Junior being born. She knew her supervisor wouldn't approve her leave, so she lied and said she had a family emergency. This would at least buy her a couple of days, including the weekend. The beauty of her being so close was Dillan Air Force Base was only a few hours away.

Brian held his son in his arms like a proud father. The more he watched Lisa cater to their son or tending to her wifely duties, the more he felt connected. It was a connection he'd never felt before. It was already nine o'clock, and their son was fed, changed, and fast asleep. She continued cleaning the kitchen while he snuck up behind her. He held her close to him.

"You are the best thing that has ever happened to me, you know that?" he said in between kisses.

"And you two are the best things that have ever happened to me," she responded while folding the wash rag and placing it over the faucet. She turned around to embrace her other half. "Now that Junior is asleep, it's time to put Brian Senior to bed as well." She smiled while leading him into the bedroom.

"Yes, I am very tired." He smiled.

Just as they reached the bedroom, the doorbell rang.

"Who is that this time of night?" he questioned cautiously. Brian was very overprotective when it came to visitors at unexpected hours. He reached for his pistol and then approached the door with caution. "Who is it?" he asked, sliding the curtain to the side.

"Your sister," said the voice. He relaxed at the sound of Monique's voice.

"It's Monique," he said, opening the door. Lisa ran to the door to greet her friend.

"Hey, big brother. I left my cell off the charger, so my battery is dead. Sorry I didn't call first," she explained and then gave Lisa a big hug.

"It's okay, I'll let you two catch up. Babe, you want me to get the air mattress out the closet?" he asked.

"Yeah." Lisa didn't even bother to look in his direction. She was happy to see her best friend.

"Anita called me as soon as that baby was born, so you know I had to find some excuse to come up here. They weren't even trying to give me leave. They act like if I leave the whole place will go to pieces." She laughed half jokingly.

"It doesn't matter. I'm just glad you are here now." Lisa hugged her again. "How long are you here for?"

"Five days. How long are you off work?"

"It was supposed to be six weeks, but I extended it to eight. I needed the time away, and I wasn't ready to send Junior to the daycare that early."

"You know you can't keep that little boy hostage forever. He will have to see the light of day sometime soon." Monique laughed at how overprotective she was. Brian slid the air mattress into the living room. "Oh, Brian, before you go, I wanted to tell you both at the same time, my boyfriend is coming to see the baby too. I think it will be good to meet him, considering we are all family. And now that she added two new additions, it's important you meet him too," she said, hoping he would be okay with the idea.

"Of course, what's his name?" he asked

"Gerard," she said proudly.

"Those two have been going strong for nearly a year," Lisa said.

"Wow, a tech school fling that actually made it past the trial period," he joked.

"He's really cool, and he loves Lisa, so you don't have to worry about him."

"You two have fun. Lisa, I'm about to go to bed." Brian waved and headed to his room

Monique waited for the door to close and then braced herself to give the bad news.

"Look, you know we are best friends. And we've been through some stuff. But I have to tell you something," Monique cautioned while Lisa anticipated the bad news.

"Don't tell me you're pregnant." She waited for Monique to continue.

"No, this is serious. I'm getting deployed to Baghdad, Iraq, for 180 days." Monique sighed.

"When?" Lisa tried to keep her composure. It seemed ever since she had the baby, she would cry at the drop of a dime. Since Monique was like her sister, it was difficult knowing her family would finally get her spotlight in the war effort.

"I go on rotation nine. We leave like in four months. I'm in the bucket, so my name got picked." She cleared her throat, preparing herself on how to break the news. "That's not the bad news. You know Gerard and Jerry are friends, right?"

"How did that happen?" Lisa shrugged her shoulders. "I don't remember bringing them around each other."

Monique shrugged her shoulders. "I guess Mr. Kennedy wasn't telling us the full truth. Before Jerry left for Hood, he came over to the dorms looking for you. Gerard was there, and I guess he was a familiar face. Next thing I know Gerard is calling me and telling me that Jerry's looking for you. Of course you know I wasn't going to let him get to you that easily."

Lisa nodded.

Monique exhaled. "Well, he's home now."

"So what?" Lisa rolled her eyes. "He's living his life, and I'm living mine. I'm happy he made it home safe, but I'm not any concern of his."

"According to Gerard, that's not true, and he's coming up this way soon as he gets released. Gerard told him the baby was here. He knows the baby's name, the engagement, everything." Monique stood up, pacing back and forth. "From what I hear, he's pretty mad."

Lisa shook her head. "Monique, what am I supposed to do, tell Brian to leave because Jerry wants to come back into the picture?"

"No, I need you to be careful. Who knows what state of mind he's in? You forget that man's job? If he was acting out before he left, I can only imagine what he's like now."

"How did he find out about this?" Lisa questioned.

"As much as I love Gerard, we don't see eye to eye with the whole Brian issue." She sat back down.

"So when is he supposed to come up here?" Lisa asked fearfully. Her life was finally back on track, and now after all this time, Jerry finally wanted to be a part of it. All she could think about was the nights spent crying because she was pregnant and alone.

"I don't know. But what I do know is Jerry is coming up here, so you better be prepared," Monique continued.

"Great, I feel so much better." She blew out a long breath of frustration. "Monique, I just got straight with Brian. Do you know what he would do to Jerry if he found out that he was watching me?"

"Something I need to know?" Brian unexpectedly interrupted. Lisa jumped and then grabbed for her chest. He was staring at the both of them waiting for an explanation.

"Brian," Lisa began, "you scared me."

"Something I need to know?" he repeated again.

Lisa thought twice about telling Brian, but she knew keeping a lie from him now after all they'd been through would only make matters worse.

"Jerry has been keeping an eye on me. When he found out that you were in our lives, supposedly he's been making threats to come up here," Lisa tried to explain, praying he wouldn't be upset with her.

"Brian, I can promise you I didn't tell him anything," Monique added.

He shook his head. "Lisa, can I see you in the bedroom?" he asked, not waiting for a response. Lisa looked at him, contemplating what his next move would be. Monique motioned to Lisa to go see what Brian wanted. She walked in the room. The moment she shut the door for some privacy, Brian went on a verbal rampage.

"If you think I'm going to allow him to come back here and mess up everything, you're wrong, Lisa!" he screamed. Lisa watched him pace back and forth. To avoid any unnecessary problems, she sat quietly, refusing to add fuel to the fire. Without warning, Brian threw back his right arm and punched the wall. Lisa couldn't take her eyes off of the damage. She could only imagine what he would do to Jerry.

"Please calm down. You know I would never do anything to jeopardize this family," Lisa whimpered.

"Lisa, if I find out he's in this house and touches my son or you, I'm putting a bullet in his head!" he shouted, rushing toward his cell phone, which was ringing nonstop. "What!" Whoever was on the phone could sense his irritability. "Yeah, man, I'll be out in a minute." Brian slammed the phone down before stuffing it in his pocket and walking toward the door. Lisa jumped up and stood before him. He watched her, anticipating her to make a move. She hugged him tightly. Startled, Brian stopped and then slowly started to calm down. He squeezed her in return.

"Brian, you don't have anything to worry about," she said, refusing to let him go.

"I love you. I don't know what I'd do if I lost you or him." He released her and then kissed her on the forehead. She smiled at his gentleness. She stared him deeply in the eyes. Her eyes told a story of a woman in love willing to fight for her family, which made Brian feel at ease. The woman in his arms was his, and no one was going to take that from him.

"Did he hit you?" Monique rushed into the bedroom.

"No, he hit the wall though." Lisa pointed to the direction of the large hole.

"Is he crazy? This is base housing. That means paperwork, jail time, loss of stripe . . . He better clean this up before you get inspected," Monique snapped with an attitude.

"I know this. We just have to get through this Jerry problem. I knew one day the truth was going to come out. I just didn't know he was going to threaten to come after me with some die-hard vengeance type madness." Lisa shook her head in disgust.

"Well don't worry, your big sister is here, and while I'm here, nothing is going to happen."

August 7, 2003

The next morning was the perfect day to do some much-needed shopping. Lisa called her lieutenant's wife, who was a stay-at-home mom, to watch Junior. When Lisa first found out she was pregnant, Lieutenant Black's wife, Melanie, became a guardian to her. Melanie adored Junior and babysat every chance Lisa needed a break. Since Monique was in town, she wanted to spend as much time with her as possible before she deployed.

While standing on the escalator in the mall, Lisa eyed each store she wanted to see. Monique, on the other hand, was looking for a place to sit down; they had been walking around the mall for almost three hours.

"I know Junior will look so cute in his new clothes." Lisa smiled at her purchase.

"You know I love you, but I am tired, so I'm going to walk over here to this food court and sit my lazy butt down. I'm starving," Monique said while walking to the nearest table.

"I'm the one that just had a baby, but you the one acting like an old lady. What's up, airman, where's your motivation?" Lisa teased.

"Right over here at this burger joint."

"All right, then let me call Brian and ask him what he wants."

While making her phone call, Lisa noticed a very attractive young woman glaring at her. She tried not to pay any mind but noticed it was becoming extremely obvious that whoever this girl was didn't care for her at all. Brushing it off as paranoia, Lisa went back over to Monique, who was already ordering her food. When she turned back around, the woman was gone.

"What's up, girl? You act like you just seen a ghost," said Monique.

"Some woman was over here staring at me like she wanted to cut me." Lisa panicked. "She's lucky I just had a baby or else I would've slapped the taste out of her mouth."

"Jealous," Monique replied while looking around for the young woman.

When they got their food, they headed outside into the parking lot, ready to leave. Lisa's phone began vibrating, and she noticed Anita was calling.

"What up, girl?" Lisa asked cheerfully.

"You tell me, Mommy," Anita teased.

"We're on our way to the base now. I'll swing by the shop."

Lisa slowly drove into the warehouse parking lot. They noticed the entire crew outside enjoying the beautiful, sunny weather. Anita wasted no time to hug both Lisa and Monique. Jasmine, on the other hand, was too busy talking and flirting with Deon.

"Didn't we get into a fight over him?" Monique questioned, staring at Deon.

"Y'all sure did," said Anita.

"That's the past. Now he dropped the last chick, so we are going to be good friends and support this relationship or fling, whatever it is." Lisa shook her head.

"Hell, she took a mighty beat down for it, we might as well," Monique joked.

"Twice." Anita laughed.

Brian greeted Lisa with a big hug. "Hello, beautiful, where's my boy?" he asked, taking his food from her.

"Ms. Melanie has him so we could go shopping."

"What you get?" he asked, curious to see what was in the bag.

"Stuff for Junior."

Jasmine ended her conversation when she noticed all her friends. She walked toward their direction with a smile on her face.

"Well if it isn't the rat pack," Jasmine joked. "Let's get some air." They walked toward the picnic bench located near the parking lot. The sun was shining, and the air was the perfect temperature for March. They piled onto a seat one by one while Jasmine pulled out a cigarette.

"Okay, what I miss?" Monique clasped her hands together, waiting for someone to respond.

"I can tell you Mister Brandon has been harassing my e-mail, you know since he doesn't have my new number," laughed Anita. "Somebody was watching over me with that one. I never thought I was going to be able to leave him."

"Yeah, you were on some serious thin line between love and psycho nonsense," Lisa agreed.

"I wonder whatever happened to that apartment," Jasmine said.

"I don't know, but did you know he drives by here three times a day and calls the shop all hours of the day? If it wasn't for Sgt. Myers having my back, he probably would've actually stopped by." Anita looked up, thanking herself for not being so weak to take him back. "I'm just glad he doesn't know where I live, or else I'd have to get a restraining order."

"You ain't lying about that, because I do live there too." Jasmine grabbed her cell phone. When she recognized the unnamed number, she grinned and quickly answered.

"What the hell?" asked Anita, staring at her with a puzzled look.

"Only good sex can make a woman that eager to answer her cell phone, considering her boyfriend is standing right over there," Monique said while pointing at Deon.

"Well we know it isn't Deon," said Anita.

When Jasmine hung up her phone, everyone was looking at her, waiting for an explanation. She smiled at her friends, knowing they were going to drill her if she didn't start talking.

"Okay, you guys, that was Alejandro." She smiled.

"Hold up, Jasmine, Alejandro Martinez?" questioned Lisa

"Yes, ma'am," she bragged.

"Wait, Jasmine, you know Alejandro and Deon don't get along," Lisa continued.

"Yeah, something like that," Jasmine replied carelessly.

"So I'm guessing that's your revenge against Deon? Date someone he doesn't like," said Monique.

"No, he's just a friend," Jasmine defended.

"Well make sure you make a list so we can keep track, 'kay?" Anita rolled her eyes.

"What about Deon?" Lisa inquired.

"What about him? In case you forgot about last year, he's far from innocent."

"No, did you forget? You were the one that got beat up twice over this man." Anita laughed.

"Funny." Jasmine rolled her eyes. "If y'all had enough of *Jasmine's Life,* I have to get back to work," Jasmine said, hugging each of them.

"Hey, let's meet at my house tonight," said Anita to all the girls.

"No can do. Between diaper changing and midnight feeding, I got a pretty hot and heavy night," Lisa replied.

"Yep, and she will probably need backup," Monique agreed.

"So just like that, I've been replaced," Jasmine joked.

On the way back to the house, Lisa noticed an unfamiliar car parked in her spot. She drove around looking for another place to park. In base housing, each resident was assigned a parking space and was limited to excess parking.

"What is this?" said Lisa, irritated. "I bet that's Sgt. Watkins's car. He is always parking in spots that don't belong to him." She thought to knock on his door but figured it was the lunch hour so he would move his car by the time she left to pick up Junior. She parked in Brian's parking spot, and both girls headed for the door. Before Lisa continued, she stopped to see Monique, who was staring at Gerard and Jerry. Lisa's heart pounded through her shirt. The man in front of her couldn't be Jerry. He still looked the same. For a split second, she remembered the emotion of loving him and the heartbreak she endured when he left.

"Hey Monique" Gerard greeted Monique. Her expression was blank.

"Gerard, what's going on?" asked Monique.

"Yeah, Gerard, what's going on?" Lisa was speechless. Jerry stood motionless. He wanted to speak to her and make the situation better, but he couldn't find the words. She was as beautiful as the day he met her.

"Hey, how about we all go inside and talk?" Gerard looked at Monique and then back at Lisa.

"Gerard, why did you bring him here?" Monique asked angrily.

"Look, let's just talk inside. Please, ladies, we don't want to make a scene out here," Gerard begged.

"No, he isn't welcome in my house, especially when my fiancé is not home," Lisa said harshly.

"Fiancé?" Jerry stormed toward Lisa and then grabbed her arm. "You have some man playing a father to a baby I didn't even know existed? You really thought I was just going to let it go?" Lisa cried hysterically for him to let her go. Monique watched in horror.

"Look, we didn't come for trouble, Lisa, we need to sit down and talk," Gerard pleaded once again.

"No, now leave before I call the police," Lisa said in between tears. She grabbed her phone and dialed for Brian. He answered on the first ring. Jerry grabbed her cell phone and threw it down on the ground. She screamed as loud as she could, hoping to get someone's attention. He covered her mouth, dragging her through the front door. Monique grabbed his arm, fighting desperately for him to let her go, but he was too strong. Gerard pulled Monique away, while Jerry shoved Lisa into the house. He pushed her to the kitchen floor so he could close the door behind him. She jumped to her feet and ran into her bedroom.

"Lisa, I just want to talk to you. We can do this without all this unnecessary crap," Jerry shouted.

"Go away, Jerry, get out of my house," she yelled from the other side of the door. She prayed silently one of the neighbors would hear her through the paper thin walls and call security forces.

"No. You can't do this to me." He punched the door as hard as he could. Lisa screamed out the loud noise. "Look, I'm sorry, I know I messed up. But believe me, I didn't know about the baby. I thought you were messing around on me, so I ended the relationship. If I would've known about the pregnancy, I would've come up here a long time ago. I wouldn't have let you go through this alone." He waited for a response, but still no answer. "Lisa, please don't do this. I still love you. I'm sorry."

He pounded on the door three more times. She could hear another man in the hallway and assumed it was Gerard. She searched around looking for her phone but remembered Jerry took it from her. Afraid to move, she could no longer hear anything from the other side of the door. She sat quietly on the floor with her arms wrapped around her legs. Ten minutes passed, but still too afraid to move, she sat curled up next to the bed until she heard Monique screaming for her to open the door. She slowly got up and turned the knob. Monique's facial expression was horrifying. She examined the marks on Lisa's arms, neck, and face.

"Is he . . ." She looked around nervously.

"He's gone. I begged Gerard to leave, so he came in here and got him, just in case one of your neighbors called security forces. He took a few of the baby's pictures you had on the wall, and looking at your hallway, you can tell there was some force going on."

Lisa sat down and shook her head. Everything Jerry said echoed in her head. Was he serious? All the pain she endured after the breakup was surfacing. She jumped when she heard two male voices coming from the back door. Monique blocked the doorway in case it was Jerry. Lisa ran to bathroom and locked herself in. She was relieved to see Brian and Deon but noticed both men were carrying their pistols in their hands.

"What's going on?" asked Brian, looking at the mess. "Where's Lisa?"

"She's in the bathroom." Brian stormed past her and knocked on the door. "I'm going to warn you, she has some marks on her," Monique continued. This only infuriated Brian.

"Lisa, it's me, open the door," he said as calmly as he could. When she opened the door, Brian could visibly see all of the marks Jerry left on her. His blood was boiling. "What happened?"

"Jerry was waiting at the door for us when we came home." Lisa's voice cracked. "He grabbed my cell phone and dragged me into the house." She wiped away each tear that fell from her eyes.

Brian's nostrils were flaring as he examined all of the damage. The pictures in the hallway were in disarray. Deon pointed to a few empty spaces where Junior's newborn pictures were once neatly placed.

"Looks like he took a couple keepsakes with him," said Deon

"Lisa, where is my son. Did he take my son?" Brian screamed.

"No, I never picked him up from Ms. Melanie." Her voice was quivering. Brian walked back into the bedroom. Lisa was shaking with fear. He hugged her, reassuring her everything was going to be okay.

CHAPTER 20

Back to Work

September 22, 2003

Sitting in the Child Development Center parking lot, Lisa looked at the building with sadness. Eight weeks flew so fast. It was time for little Junior to start his first day without his mother. She wasn't prepared to leave him just yet but knew the day was coming sooner or later. She took a moment before taking off her seatbelt and reaching for Junior. He sat in his car seat looking at his mother. She adored his tiny features, but oddly enough, when she saw her child, she saw Jerry. Junior was almost a spitting image of his biological father.

"Come on, Pumpkin, time to go." She sighed. In one quick swoop, she lifted his carrier in one hand and his baby bag in the other. When she walked through the door, she was greeted by the receptionist, who explained where his room was located. Lisa followed the instructions carefully and then entered the room. The moment she walked in, she saw other tiny babies sitting in bouncers and cribs and laying on changing tables.

"Hello, you must be Brian's mommy," the young woman greeted.

"Yes." Lisa smiled back. *Yes, I am his mommy, and if anything happens to my baby, I'll see to it you will never make it to prom.* Lisa couldn't help but notice how young she looked, and why was she taking care of newborns?

"My name is Sandy. And this is where little Brian will be taking his naps, so if you have a blanket or something that you would like to bring in, please feel free to do so," she said pointing to the empty crib next to the window. "We will need three bottles with his name on them. We provide regular Enfamil and cereal. If he's on a special diet, you will need to provide the formula. Other than that, you can just provide the bottles," she continued on.

"Okay. Thanks." Lisa carried out each instruction and then headed to the door, leaving her baby for the first time. Each step was harder and harder. As much as she wanted to turn back, she knew she had to get to work.

When Lisa walked in, she was greeted by friends and coworkers waiting to see baby pictures. She presented each one proudly.

"Welcome back, Mommy," Sgt. Myers greeted.

"Thank you, ma'am."

"Now since you are back, here is a list of things I need you to take care of for me. First and foremost, we have eleven pages of bench stock that needs to be pulled out of the warehouse. Second, the put-away items are overflowing, so I know for a fact Garcia will need your help on that," Sgt. Myers continued.

"Wait, who?" Lisa didn't recognize the name. "A new person?"

"Yeah and he is quite the looker. Only problem is, he knows it," Anita chimed in.

"He's a Senior Airman, came from Seymour Johnson AFB down in South Carolina." Sgt. Myers pointed to the young man lifting boxes into the warehouse.

"I'll get right on it." Lisa grabbed all the bench stock labels and walked to the warehouse, eyeing Garcia. Even she had to admit he was pretty good looking. Brian would probably have a fit if he caught her staring this hard. Luckily he was too involved in his work to notice her stare down.

"Something caught your eye?" Jasmine caught her off guard.

"Huh? No. I was daydreaming. It just so happens I was looking in his direction." Lisa tried to think of an excuse as to why she was staring so hard.

"Yeah, whatever." Jasmine laughed.

"I'm taken," Lisa said, grabbing a cart.

"Make sure you remember that too, because Brian will beat that man down if he even thought you were having ideas of messing around," Jasmine warned.

After everything was sent over to vehicle dispatcher, Lisa went over to help Garcia. She was trying not to look so obvious, but something about him attracted her. Whatever it was, she knew she had to snap out of it before someone caught her and word got back to Brian.

"Airman Collier, I need to talk to you for a moment," Sgt. Myers called from inside the office.

"Yes, ma'am, what can I do for you?" she asked, walking through the door.

"There is no easy way of saying this to you, so I'm just going to be upfront."

"Okay, did I do something wrong?" Lisa pondered.

"We have two airmen selected for the next rotation. You and Airman Garcia." Sgt. Myers's facial expression was blank, matching Lisa's.

"What do you mean next rotation? That's in three months." Lisa questioned, "Where am I going?"

"Al Udeid Air Base, Qatar."

"Ma'am, I just had a baby." She stopped herself before her tone got any louder. "You mean to tell me you are deploying me five months after I gave birth to my son?"

"I know how you feel, but you are coming up on the red list, and you do have an obligation. Trust me, Lisa, I know how you feel, but think of it like this: get it over while he is still young so he won't remember. It's only 120 days."

"Sgt. Myers, 120 days is a long time. Please don't make me do this," Lisa begged. "What is the air force regulation about new parents and deployments? Isn't there a waiting period?"

"Yes, there is, six months. By the time you ship out, your son will just be hitting that mark," Sgt. Myers said.

Lisa nodded slowly.

"Look, Collier, it's out of my hands. Be happy you have enough time to get everything straight now. You know if you weren't on this deployment, you were putting yourself at risk for those long-term tours. I'm talking about 365 days to Iraq," she continued.

"Yes, ma'am."

"Now, I already told Airman Garcia, so I want you two to get together and coordinate out processing schedules."

Lisa didn't respond. The last thing she wanted to do was leave her son or Brian. There was no right or wrong time to tell him, so now was the best. She reached for her phone and dialed his number.

October 23, 2003

It had been almost two months, and Gerard still had not called Monique. She began to wonder where their relationship stood. The confusion was becoming almost too much to bear. She picked up her cell phone to dial his number.

"Hello?" the raspy voice said.

"Hey, baby, what are you doing?" Her voice was shaky.

"Not much, sitting here. I haven't heard from you in a while. I was beginning to think you dropped off the face of the earth."

"Gerard, communication is a two-way street."

"You right." He paused for a moment, letting out a loud sigh. "I missed you," he admitted. Monique grinned. "Stop smiling. You know I can hear you through the phone," he joked.

"Shut up," she said playfully. "Um, I'll be leaving in a month, and I was just curious if maybe we can arrange for some leave time."

"I think I might like that."

"Okay, well I'll be taking a week off before I go, so maybe I can catch a flight up there?"

"Yeah, that would be nice. You need any money for the ticket? I know that's kind of pushing it."

"No, Gerard, I'm okay. I just want to see you."

They continued their conversation, never once mentioning Jerry or Lisa. Monique was just happy to talk to her love. After an hour of chitchat, they made their plans for her going away and ended the conversation.

CHAPTER 21

Off to War

November 12, 2003

Monique could feel the plane lifting off the ground. She sat back in her chair with her headphones on. The music took her mind off of her destination. There was no secret about possible deployments to anywhere. In this profession, you were trained for the purpose of fighting and defending at all costs, even if that meant separating from everyone you hold dear for months on end. Memories of her time with Gerard replayed in her mind. They both decided to spend their leave in Las Vegas gambling and drinking. She toyed with memories of the two getting married in her head. The flight was scheduled to land in Germany for a nine-hour layover and then off to the desert life. A little bit of fear sat in her stomach while she watched the land slowly disappear out of her window. All the training she endured before her departure made her realize that what she was getting herself into was real, and she was no longer viewing it from the comfy seat in her living room. She was okay with the idea of performing supply details, but when they were told that convoys was a part of the job description, reality hit them like a lightning bolt. In most cases, they would ship out on C130 aircraft along with the air crew, but since Monique was flying solo, she was allowed to fly commercial.

The plane quickly jerked as it attempted to land, awakening Monique from her sleep. She looked around, watching other passengers preparing to gather their things. She looked out the window and saw the flight line to Ramstein AFB. From her view, it didn't look like much. She only wished she could see what the hype was about Germany. Everyone she came in contact with always spoke highly of Ramstein AFB and Sembach AFB. It was said the per diem was high and the tour sites were gorgeous. Unfortunately, she wouldn't get to experience either one unless she was able to change duty stations. *What am I supposed to do with myself for nine hours?* The airport was filled with military in uniform waiting for their flight home or to their next destination. Hoping to recognize someone she may have known from Lackland or Andrews, she continued through the crowd, looking around for familiar faces.

November 13, 2003

Lisa sat quietly, waiting for Brian to arrive home. It was already three o'clock in the morning, and he hadn't texted or called all night. She wondered where this deployment left their relationship. Ever since she'd told him, he'd started acting differently toward her, always hanging out with other women at night and standing her up for lunch dates. People always said the military lifestyle could tear a happy couple apart, but she couldn't believe their relationship would ever suffer. Junior's cry disturbed her deep thought. She ran to her little boy's side. He stared at her with Jerry's charming eyes. She couldn't understand how someone she loved so deeply could resemble someone she hated. The gleam in his eye told her he knew what he was doing and he knew who she was. She picked him up and kissed him on the cheek.

"Hey, baby, you knew Mommy would come get you." She laughed. As she walked toward the room, she heard the front door slam. Immediately she knew it was Brian. She laid Junior back into the bassinet and proceeded to the living room. Brian had obviously been drinking.

"Brian, have you lost your mind? It's three in the morning," she said. Brian was hardly fazed by her tone.

"I know what time it is. I can read," he snapped in between slurs. "Now, how 'bout we go in the bedroom and get some sleep. I'm tired." He continued walking toward her.

"No, you come up in this house all hours of the night, drunk, and think I'm supposed to sleep with you?" she snapped. "Sleep out in the living room." She stopped and then turned back to face him. "Is this how you're going to be when I'm deployed? You are supposed to be taking care of Junior." She attempted to walk away, but Brian grabbed her arm forcefully.

"Are you trying to say I'm not a responsible father? Like I don't know how to take care of my own son?" he yelled, close range to her face.

"Brian, you are drunk, and you don't know what you are doing. Let me go," she said in between her clenched teeth.

"What you care? You're going to be too busy messing with other guys in the desert anyway." He chuckled. "Why do you care about me or Junior?" He laughed while releasing his grip and walking over to the couch.

"Is that what you think, Brian?"

He shrugged his shoulders nonchalantly.

"Well think again. You think I want to leave my baby?" She shook her head at the man in front of her. "You act like I'm not upset. I just . . ." His cell phone cut her off.

"Hello?" he answered.

Lisa could hear a female voice on the other end. She crossed her arms with her eyebrows raised. He looked up at her and could tell she wasn't happy with what was going on.

"Yeah, I made it home safe. Thanks for checking up." He closed the phone.

"Is that another woman that just called your phone, Brian?" she yelled.

"Stop screaming before you wake up Junior," he responded, unaffected by her anger.

"Brian, you don't even care how this affects me or your son." She could hardly continue. "You want to cheat? I'll show you cheating." She continued walking toward the kitchen.

"What!" he yelled while running behind her. He grabbed her and shook her forcefully. "If you even think about cheating on me, I will kill anyone you even think about touching."

"Let . . . me . . . go." She tried to break free, but his grip was too strong. He continued cursing and shaking her. When she saw his face, he didn't look like himself. There was something different about him.

"I'm not playing, Lisa." He finally let her go. She reached over for the pot on the stove and swung it at his head as hard as she could. He fell to the floor in pain as she continued to hit him over and over again.

"Don't you ever put your hands on me," she finally let out, walking to her cell phone to call security forces. In less than ten minutes, they were already taking Brian into custody. She grabbed Junior and headed for Anita's.

November 15, 2003

Once Monique stepped off the plane, the dry heat slapped her in her face. It was 104 degrees, and she could barely breathe.

"Oh, man," she yelled. Monique knew Baghdad was going to be hot in the summertime, but she didn't think it would be this bad. "I can't breathe."

"All you have to do is open your mouth. You'll get used to it." The voice behind her laughed. Monique turned to see a young girl standing behind her. "Is this your first time here?" she asked.

Monique nodded. There was nothing but sand as far as her eyes could see. Tent city was just that—hundreds of tents lined in a row in front of a giant airport. Each tent was labeled and marked appropriately.

"Don't worry, you'll get used to it." The girl grabbed her bag and headed to the back of the aircraft.

"Form a cargo line, let's go," screamed a husky technical sergeant with a whistle in his hand.

"A what?" asked Monique.

"We have to form a line to take all the bags off the plane," the girl answered.

"Oh." They all gathered together for further instruction and then continued with the baggage. Monique could barely function from jet lag.

Once all the bags were taken off, the passengers were escorted to the main hangar for their in-processing briefing. Monique felt like she was in hell. Not only was it hot, but she also had to listen to someone talk for an hour straight about stuff she was going to forget anyway.

"Why do they do this to us?" Monique asked the stranger she'd met on the plane.

"I wish I knew. You know how it is—shut up and color." She laughed. "Leslie," she blurted.

"Monique." She shook the girl's hand. "Normally I'm a little bit livelier than this, but this jet lag has me out of my norm."

"Don't worry, this is as good as it gets with me," Leslie responded.

"Works for me."

Monique and Leslie fought their sleep until the briefing was over. They proceeded to nearby tent labeled "Females 105" and laid their belongings on the first cot closest to the exit.

"Wow, so this is desert life, huh?" asked Monique, looking around her new home.

"Yes, ma'am, welcome to the Sandbox," a girl nearby answered.

"I'm hungry. Anyone want to join me at the chow tent? The TCNs make a mean omelet," said Leslie to no one in particular.

"TCNs?" Monique asked.

"Third country nationals," they all replied in unison.

"What time is it?" one of the girls asked.

"I have no idea. Something has to be open. The sun is out, and so is half the base," Leslie responded.

"We have to wear PT gear all the time?" Monique asked, reading the introduction packet they received upon arrival.

"Yes, ma'am, PT clothing or standard military issued. No civilian attire, ladies. Remember, we are at war fighting for our country, so showing off the goodies is an absolute no-no," Leslie preached.

"There goes my morale," one of the other women responded.

All the girls complied, and in less than twenty minutes they were all ready and heading for the chow hall. Monique was amazed at all the tents and hangars. She'd never been out of the States. They maneuvered through the buildings, locating the gym and the BX. Even though all the ladies were dressed in blue and gray military PT gear, they all strutted with pride, catching a few head turns as they passed. Monique couldn't believe all the attention she was getting. This was a lot more than she was used to in the States. She would have to put on the tightest outfit and fix her hair to an uptight hairstyle in order to get the entire base to look her way like this.

"What are we, in prison?" Monique joked.

Leslie and the others just laughed. "Oh, I keep forgetting you're new. Check this out. One of the things you are going to learn is that you are a ten in the States, right?" Leslie questioned.

Monique wondered why she was asking such a strange question. "I guess, why?"

"Well," Leslie began as she looked around the area, "you see girlfriend over there?" She pointed to an average-looking female wearing too much makeup. With all of the heat, her face looked like it was going to melt.

Monique nodded.

"That, my friend is what we call a Desert Queen," Leslie continued, while Monique raised an eyebrow. "Let me explain. In the States she's rates on average, a five. Over here, where men are desperate and deprived, she is a ten. You see, she will do anything for these guys as long as they show her the attention she lacks at home."

"Um, okay, so what does that have to do with us?" Monique wasn't following.

"In the States you are a dime, so over here you are a quarter, maybe even a dollar." Leslie winked and waved the girls to keep walking.

All the girls entered the chow hall tent, grabbing a tray and silverware.

December 3, 2003

It had been almost two months since Brian and Lisa had separated. It was almost time for her deployment, and they were nowhere near reconciling. She spent most of her time with the new airman getting to know each other and planning their out-processing. Lisa could barely fathom the idea of parting from her baby but knew this could happen. Brian moved back in with Deon while they shared custody. The phone rang, nearly causing her to jump out of her seat.

"Hello," she said, trying to focus her eyes on the clock. It was 1:00 a.m. when Junior woke her up for his late-night feeding.

"Hey, beautiful, you busy?" Brian asked sincerely. This was the usual when he got drunk with his friends. He would call countless times during the night, pleading for Lisa to take him back. Normally she would've just shrugged him off, but by now she had started to pity him.

"Hey, Brian." She sounded uninterested.

"My son awake?" he asked. This was unusual; she could tell he wasn't drunk at all. The sober tone in his voice almost sounded like hope.

"Yeah, but I'm going to put him back to bed because I don't want his schedule off."

"Well, you tell him Daddy can't wait to get him tomorrow."

"I will, Brian." She looked at the phone, confused. "Goodnight."

She closed her phone and continued back to her son. The next day seemed like the norm. It was just another day in the storage and issue office. Anita and Jasmine were almost inseparable, while Lisa spent her free time with Garcia.

"Garcia!" Lisa screamed as she was coming out of the office into the warehouse.

"Call me Juan." He laughed. He really liked her, and the last thing he wanted was the boundaries of the last-name basis.

"Sorry . . . *Juan.*" She giggled. "What's on the agenda?"

"Medical," he said. "Maybe dinner?"

"What?" She looked surprised. "Juan, you know my situation. A single mommy dating right now so close to deployment. I'll pass."

"C'mon, we're friends, right? Plus we are about to embark on a 120-day journey together. So there is no excuse out here. Let's just enjoy all the American food we can together." He winked.

"What is it with me around very persistent men?" She laughed to herself.

"Well I don't know about all that, but I do know that we leave in six days and I'm ready to enjoy the American life while I can, because I know for a fact I'm going to miss Red Lobster." He was nearly drooling.

"Oh and the cheese biscuits, yummy," she thought out loud.

"Great I'll pick you up at seven."

"Uh, no dating for me." She shrugged off the idea.

"How do you know I'm even interested in you?"

Lisa shot him a look of confusion but realized what he meant.

"I go out to eat with my friends all the time. It doesn't mean I'm dating them." He laughed.

"All right, wise guy, since this isn't a date, I'll meet you there." She sucked her teeth.

"Darn, you can't even be a gentleman and pick me up?" he asked, pretending to be hurt.

"Oh, shut up, Garcia."

They continued their flirtatious conversation until Juan noticed Brian walking toward him and Lisa.

"Hey, your pit bull is here. I'm out," he mumbled. Juan and Brian had had a few confrontations since Lisa mentioned the deployment almost two months ago. Even though the two were broken up, Brian was very jealous and made it known Lisa was off limits.

"Where's your man going? I just came to say hi," interrupted Brian sarcastically.

"Brian, shut up." Lisa refused to entertain Brian's childish behavior. The last thing she would ever do was give him the satisfaction of the day. She walked into the warehouse.

"So am I still on for my son tonight?" He asked with a Kool-Aid smile.

She turned around, giving him the look of death. It was almost the same look she gave him when they first met.

"Brian, what is your angle?" She crossed her arms. "You know good and well you're getting your son tonight, so what's up with this?" She motioned around.

He looked at her with anger. "Fine, I just came to see how you're doing, but I see I'm bothering you. I guess I'll call my girlfriend, because she surely is the only female here that knows how to treat a man." He popped open his phone, hoping his actions was making her jealous. "Oh that's right. You have a new man in your life now. You aren't worried about me" He shook his head.

"Okay, well while you call your girlfriend, I have to get back to work." She grabbed her cart and walked away. She wasn't surprised. He and the mistress who was checking on him that horrible night magically became his girlfriend less than a week later. It didn't matter to her because she knew where his heart was. Brian was a little irritated she didn't have a snappy comeback for him. It was almost as if she was over him. That was the last thing he wanted. He had Amanda now, but she could never give him what Lisa gave him. Their relationship was rocky, but it wasn't over, at least not in Brian's eyes.

It was almost 7:00 p.m., and Lisa was already dressed and waiting for Brian to come get Junior. She decided to wear her hair out. Tonight she was going to be sexy. It had been almost a year since she remembered what it felt like to be beautiful. It was warm out, so she kept it simple and cute: tight jeans with a plain black tight tee and matching black pumps. Since Junior was born, she was magically blessed with implant-like breasts. She sprayed her Charlie White and popped open her favorite lip gloss. The doorbell finally rang, and she quickly gathered all of hers and Junior's things. Once she opened the door, Brian's eyes nearly popped out of his head. Lisa was just as gorgeous as the day he met her.

"Hey." His voice shook a little.

"Hey." She tried not to look in his eyes. Regardless of the pain she felt, she still loved him deeply. "Well, you wanted him, you got him." She turned her attention back to her son.

When he reached for Junior, his hand slid across her stomach, nearly intensifying the butterflies in her belly. Embarrassed, Lisa tried to avoid contact. He looked at her again and then leaned over, kissing her lips softly. Lisa stood there remembering what it felt like to be with him again. Magic.

Lisa stepped back with a weak smile. "Brian, I have to go."

"Where you going?" He looked defeated.

"Red Lobster. I'm meeting a friend." She shut the door and locked it behind her.

"Garcia." Brian didn't have to be a mind reader to know she was going out with him.

"I'll pick Junior up Sunday." Without a word to her other half, she walked to her car, refusing to look back. She could almost feel the burning stare on her back. The moment she hopped in the car, she quickly sped off, hoping he hadn't seen the tears coming down her face.

The dinner was everything she needed and wanted. *120 days in the desert with this man is going to be a challenge,* she thought. Not only was Juan a good friend, but he was also exactly what she needed to get over Brian. When she got home, she could see the lights were on in the house. Brian's car was still in the parking lot. Fear trembled in her heart. *Lord, please don't let him try anything stupid.* She slowly walked through the kitchen, and there were candles lit everywhere. *What the . . .* Junior was sitting contently in his booster seat. He was completely surrounded with rose petals and pillows. She ran toward her son, confused. His smile made her relax a little. When she picked him up, she read his shirt: *Please forgive my daddy.*

"Oh, my goodness," she said out loud, looking around the room. The rose petals were all over the floor leading to the bathroom. She pushed the door slightly open and saw the bubble bath waiting for her. The petals continued into the bedroom, where Brian waited, patiently dressed from head to toe.

"Brian, what's going on?" she questioned.

"I destroyed us. Now I want to fix us," he said, pointing to the room. "Let me be your man again and make this right between us." He smiled.

"Hello? Did you forget something?" she said, pointing to Junior. "We have our son here, and he doesn't look like he's going to bed anytime soon."

"Who said we had to do anything?"

She gave him a twisted look.

"I just want to enjoy what little time we have left together."

CHAPTER 22

Desert Life

December 18, 2003

onique was excited about being in the desert. The heat felt like it could choke a horse, but the excitement of being away from home brought a smile to her face. She walked through tent city, thinking about her family and what they were doing. Her thoughts were interrupted by a loud giggle coming from a nearby tent. Leslie poked her head through doorway, looking both ways for any authority figures. When the coast was clear, she slipped out as fast as she could.

"What's up?" asked Leslie, walking toward her with a little bit of a limp.

"Are you okay?" Monique couldn't help but notice her limp.

"I'm good, Sgt Jennings was teaching me some martial arts moves and I think he sprained something in my back." She rubbed her back.

"Sgt. Jennings? Isn't he married?" Monique questioned.

"Yeah, what's your point? It's not like we did anything," she snapped.

"Martial arts, huh?" Monique asked with both eye brows raised.

"Isn't that what I said? I have twelve other witnesses if you need me to prove it." Leslie defended.

"Okay, I believe you" She could tell she wasn't going to win this argument. "So where you headed?" Monique changed the subject.

"Sleep. My back hurts," Leslie whimpered.

"I guess fooling around on cots is a no-go on my list," Monique snickered.

December 19, 2003

The next morning was a typical day for Monique. Every morning was the same, rushing to the "bathroom" for her three-minute shower and brushing her teeth with bottled water just so she wouldn't develop any strange disease from the faucet. She was almost nervous to take a shower. Her flip flops hitting the sand and rocks made a loud clacking noise. The annoying sound made it hard to enjoy the pleasant desert life. Once she made it to the latrine, she noticed a camel scoping around the area.

"Oh, goodness, Fred, can I ever get a day off from you?" She rushed past, hoping he wouldn't follow her.

Fred was almost like family to the members of the base. Security forces even took the liberty of giving him his own access badge so he could maneuver on and off the installation. Although keeping Fred as a pet was unauthorized, the top dogs on base were rarely around to even notice the beast scoping out the area. He was a nasty creature who had a habit of spitting and sitting where he didn't belong. It was almost as if he believed he was a member of the armed forces just like the others. Normally Fred was only allowed to wander near the front gate. It was a mystery how he was able to get so close to the women's area. Monique shook her head at the funny-shaped thing. She ran by one of the packaged water crates and grabbed six bottles of water. After taking a quick, almost-pointless shower, she headed off to work.

She stepped into the oversized hangar, which contained eleven hummers spilling out onto the flight line.

"Hernandez, what's all this?" Monique asked one of her closest comrades.

"Humanitarian mission. Something us air force folks can only go on as long as the army is babysitting. You know, so we feel like real soldiers," he responded sarcastically, placing the clipboard on the first vehicle.

"Humanitarian mission? I thought those have to be preapproved, and last time I checked my chain of command didn't tell me a thing about a mission." Monique was confused.

"Who do you think brought these here?" He pointed to the hummers.

"Ay, Grant, you riding with the MPs in the fifth truck," Sgt. Anthony Rogers interrupted. It was no secret Rogers had a crush on Monique but was too afraid to approach her. Rogers was an olive-skinned man who wore a clean-cut shave and had beautiful brown eyes. He had a few options, but he wanted Monique. From the moment they stepped foot off the plane they were almost inseparable. Considering her long history with Gerard, she made it a point to let everyone know she was taken. The strong bond held between the two was unbreakable and hard to compete with.

"Which one are you riding in?" Hernandez asked Rogers.

"With my girlfriend, what do you think?" Rogers laughed. "Grant, strap up at the armory and get your gear. You got twenty minutes." He continued turning to Hernandez. "Brother, I've been trying to get her attention for a month now."

"Rog, you my boy. You got that in the bag. I say make your move. It's not like she's going anywhere else for the next eleven hours." Hernandez flashed his award-winning smile.

"No, man, from what I hear, she's committed." Rogers shook his head in defeat. "No home wrecking on my part."

"I wouldn't put too much on that, brother, she hasn't called him once since she's been here," Hernandez continued.

Hernandez was in the Puerto Rican National Guard working in vehicle maintenance. There wasn't a woman on the entire installation who wouldn't give him the time of day. Unlucky for all of them, he was one of the few faithful men to his girlfriend back home. She was definitely model material.

Once Monique had all of her gear, it was time to ride. This wasn't her first time outside of theater; she'd experience three since she first landed. The commander made it a point for each person to experience Iraq at least once during their deployment. Once or twice a month a convoy of army and air force would travel through the nearby cities handing out clothes, medical supplies, and other basic needs. Anything needed to support the mission. She said a silent prayer as she stepped into the truck. These missions were meant to support the Iraqi people, but it wasn't uncommon to come into contact with insurgents. Prayer and letters from home were her only escape from her shaken reality. A day hadn't gone by when Monique wasn't faced with a bombing or mortar attack on base, so each time they drove off, she kept her Bible and cross tightly in her hand. Dressing in full gear almost became second nature. Rogers entered the hummer, breaking Monique out of deep thought. She enjoyed being with him because as silly as it might sound, she felt protected. He lifted her hand with a smile.

"Did you say a prayer for us?" he asked nervously. Rogers was never much of a religious person, but when it came to his life, he was willing to be a part of anyone's prayer chain.

"You know it," Monique returned a half smile.

As soon as the vehicles started, Monique felt her stomach flipping inside-out. She hated this part of her job. Baghdad was no stranger to bombs going off, but when they drove out of the wire, there was no longer a feeling of partial safety but more so of fear. At this moment, her mind slipped into mechanical mode; no thinking, just doing. That might mean firing back at someone shooting at you or running to the nearest shelter in place to avoid a gas attack or ambush. The horror stories of prisoner of war victims in war camps gave the troops a feeling captivity was not an option. If they were going down, they were going all the way. After an hour, they finally entered one of the nearby cities. Monique could see children running next to her truck. She smiled at the thought of her and Gerard having kids. Her smile vanished when one of them made a shooting gesture with his forefinger and thumb. The oxygen slowly exhaling from her mouth helped ease her nerves. A tear slowly fell down her cheek as she imagined a grenade being thrown from the top of one of the buildings or a bomb exploding from a child's backpack as he approached a military soldier for a piece of candy. In one quick second, all the vehicles came to a halt. Rogers jerked from his seat nervously, scanning his surroundings. This made Monique uneasy; they never stopped in the middle of the city. It was too dangerous. They could see people exiting from the first two trucks.

"What is going on?" Monique asked out loud.

"I don't know, but I'm about to find out," he said as he exited the hummer.

Monique sat in the vehicle as she watched the four men cluster together, pointing at one of the buildings. After five minutes, they dispersed back to their assigned stations. Rogers looked distraught.

"What's up?" Monique wasted no time to ask.

"Checking for insurgents, I guess." Rogers shook his head.

"Are you kidding me?" Monique was ready to shoot her fellow wingmen. "As loud as these trucks are, I'm pretty sure those guys heard us coming twenty minutes ago. If this is anything like my old neighborhood, they would've gone out the back long before we could be hot on their trails."

"One of the locals jumped out in front of the first vehicle complaining about something. I don't even think the translators could understand him." Rogers studied the surrounding area.

"Since when did we reclass to Security?" Monique shook her head.

"Welcome to the military," Rogers said while looking around the other vehicles.

Monique stepped out of the vehicle while keeping an eye on the people around her. In her mind, no one could be trusted. Everyone looked suspicious, from scowling stares from men dressed in all white to women in all black burqaas covered from head to toe. Young children danced around the vehicles, playing and carrying on. She held on tightly to her M4A1 weapon. The tan-colored buildings were all made of concrete. The poverty-stricken neighborhood was flooded with sick and wounded civilians. Many of them were hit in cross fires, while others suffered from lack of food and water. Monique noticed the women nearby staring at her. The piercing eyes behind the covered faces gave her goose bumps. Each one whispered to one another, as if they shared a secret no one knew. It was only a matter of time before someone made a move, and she made sure to be ready. All of the times she came to the villages, she never had an issue until now. Something was not right. One woman in particular studied Monique's every move. In a weird way, it was almost as if the young girl was secretly calling for help. *Why is she staring at me?* Monique could see splattered blood on her cover. *Is it hers? Is she okay?* Her eyes widened and mouth dropped.

"Hey . . ." She waved to the girl. Startled, the little girl ran back into the alleyway where she had been standing. Monique tried to give chase, but the girl was too fast. As she approached the dimly lit area, she thought twice about going after her. *What if she's in trouble?* Monique waited patiently, hoping the girl would reappear. She flashed a little light to gain some visibility. The girl was nowhere in sight.

"Hello!" Monique screamed.

"Hey," Rogers interrupted behind her.

Monique jumped. She quickly turned her attention back into the house.

"Are you okay?" Rogers grabbed her face to look at him. "You don't look too good."

"No." She turned back to the direction the young girl was standing and then noticed the trail of blood. "I mean, I'm fine. I thought I saw something."

"The desert got you seeing things now?" Rogers laughed and then pulled her back to the direction of the truck. "Come on, we're going to head back to the base."

"What about the supplies?" Monique pointed to the trucks. "That's the reason we came out here, right? I did not spend hours packing pillows and blankets into that truck just to turn back around," Monique crossed her arms.

"Grant, they found three of our translators upstairs. They were shot execution style. We don't know who or what, but what we do know is we have to go."

December 23, 2003

The plane ride was long and almost unbearable. Lisa could barely get so much of an ounce of sleep. The layover in Kuwait wasn't as comfortable as she thought it would be. Forty-two service men and women raced through the airport in wheelchairs to help pass the time while the other half attempted to sleep in sleeping bags on the cold floor. After what seemed to be an eternity in the air, they finally landed. There was a seven-hour time difference from Delaware to Qatar, and jet lag was already settling in.

"Bag line," screamed an unknown man standing next to everyone's luggage.

"Ah shut up, I'm coming," Lisa mumbled to herself.

Once Lisa made it to her tent, she found the nearest empty cot and crashed. Ever since her date with Juan, she was overwhelmed with confusion. Brian had made every attempt to win her back. She was a fool not to take him back, but something about Juan sparked her interest. Brian begged her to marry him before she left. After numerous attempts, she gave in, and they were married no less than a week later. This deployment was not only going to be a test for their marriage but also on their family. The empty feeling without her son was dragging the life out of her. She felt like a horrible mother. If he woke up in the middle of the night searching for a familiar face, she wasn't going to be there. *Will he remember this?* The pictures couldn't fill the void of the absence, but this was her job. *If the military wanted you to have a family, they would've issued you one.* The words from her fellow comrades echoed in her mind. When she explained she would be leaving her son for four months, people gave her the third degree that a mother's place is with her child and not in a man's war. This wasn't the 1950s; times were different. A woman deserves to represent her country and be called a hero just like any other.

December 24, 2003

The morning didn't look too promising for Lisa. She wasn't feeling the 120-degree summer heat, and they weren't able to start their duties until their chief arrived. In the meantime, this gave her and Garcia free time to check out their new home. Deployment was a new experience for Lisa. She had never been outside of the United States a day in her life, and for her to travel to another country and see people from all over the world was very exciting. The base was filled with all branches from every service of the United States, and with soldiers from countries including Australia and England. The Australian Air Force traveled in their own pack and barely associated with anyone outside their group. The Qatar military barely spoke much English and associated mostly with security forces or the military members from Uganda.

"They decide to send us here just days before Christmas," Lisa whined. "I wonder how they celebrate the holidays around here." Lisa looked around for any signs of life.

"Beats me," Garcia joked.

They walked towards a set of tables and chairs neatly set underneath a large tent.

"This must be the morale tent I keep hearing about." Garcia shook his head. "You got your beer card?"

"Yeah, why, you want it?" Lisa asked, pulling it out of her pocket. "I don't drink."

"Can you believe we are restricted to three alcoholic beverages a day? I'm surely going to sober up now."

"Well I guess they just served their purpose now, didn't they?" She smiled. "You better be glad you aren't up north because my friend Monique just told me they aren't allowed any alcohol." Lisa smiled. "From what I hear, guys are getting drunk off of mouthwash and cough medicine."

"Forget that," Garcia said as he watched a man approach the two. "If a grown man is going to fight a war, he should be able to sit back and relax with a nice cold beer when he gets home."

Lisa shook her head.

"What's up, folks?" the tall, lanky man mustered before sitting himself down next to Lisa uninvited.

"Nothing, brother, just trying to figure out what to do on this base," Garcia responded.

"Well you know we got the beer tent, where you sitting at now. The club is open every night thanks to DJ Fresh, my homeboy from North Carolina. We're having a big blowout holiday celebration tonight." The stranger smiled widely. "What's good, girl? What's your name?" He gave his attention to Lisa. Garcia chuckled at the funny man's attempt.

"Collier, yours?" she greeted.

"I guess you can't read your name tape, Roberts," Garcia joked.

Lisa looked down at her blouse as if she'd forgotten she'd changed her name. She still wasn't used to the idea of being married.

"What's your name?" Lisa rolled her eyes.

"Rottweiler, or you can call me by my government, Michael Jenkins."

"Okay, Jenkins." Lisa tried to finish without laughing. "What kind of nickname is Rottweiler?"

"Because I'm cute, but if you test me, I'll bite you." He jumped, emulating an attack.

"Oh."

"I should have been called Diamond, because I'm every woman's best friend." He winked.

Lisa was clearly not impressed with his jokes.

"Ah, got it. Hey, Garcia, I think it's time to head back now. What you think?" She pointed to her nonexistent watch on her wrist.

"You know what, I am kind of sleepy, and since I'm on the twelve-hour night shift, I guess I better catch some z's before my first day of work," Garcia agreed as both exited the table.

"It was nice meeting you, Mr. Rottweiler." Lisa smiled back at the strange gentleman.

"I guess I'll catch you at the club tonight!" Jenkins raised his hand in the air, signaling a peace sign before walking in the opposite direction.

"Who goes to a club on a Wednesday night before Christmas?" Lisa asked with a confused look.

"Us," Garcia said and smiled.

"Huh?" She shook her head. "I don't think so."

"Why not? You don't have a job, and we have nothing to do until the Chief gets here," Garcia responded.

She shook her head at his persistence. "Whatever, I'm going to make a phone call. I'll catch you later." She waved and walked away.

"Don't forget two fifteen-minute phone calls a week; don't waste them all in the same day," Garcia warned.

Lisa walked toward the media center, contemplating whether or not she should call Brian. She had only been there two days and already she was feeling homesick. If she was going to make it, she knew she had to do something to occupy herself for the next four months. After ten minutes of debating, she decided to call her mother. If there was anyone she could rely on to make her feel better, it was her. After walking into the building and signing in, she was pointed to a phone near the exit. Once she was seated, she read the instructions and proceeded with her call.

"Fort Belvoir, operator twenty," the operator said.

"Yes, I would like to make a morale call."

After explaining all the detailed deployment information, the operator finally transferred the call. The phone rang, but there was no answer. It hurt because she knew the next time she would talk to her was later in the week. The next person was Brian. He answered on the first ring.

"Hello." He sounded sleepy.

"Hey, Brian, did I wake you?" She sounded relieved to hear a familiar voice.

"Not at all. As a matter of fact, your son is sitting next to me waiting to hear from his mommy." He laughed. "Hold on, I'll put the phone up to his ear."

After a few minutes of shuffling, she could hear her baby breathing heavily on the phone. A knot formed in the back of her throat. She could barely talk. It took everything in her not to burst into tears.

"Hey, Junior . . ." She paused as the tears forced their way down her face. "Mommy misses you so much. I love you." She waited, as if he could respond. "I'll be home soon, I promise."

The cooing sounds made her heart beat faster. She put her head on the table as she held the phone tightly in her hand. She didn't even notice Brian was back on the phone.

"Don't worry, baby, I'll send plenty of pictures, and I'll make sure he doesn't forget his mommy."

Lisa didn't answer, and he hadn't expected her to.

"You can do this. Merry Christmas, my love," he continued.

"Thanks, hubby. I don't know what I'd do without you. Merry Christmas."

They talked for a little while until the desk clerk shouted, "One minute left."

"Baby, I have to go," she said, letting out a few more tears.

"Bye, Lisa. We'll be sitting here waiting for your next call," he said, hanging up the phone.

She sat back in the chair staring at the wall; she collected herself and walked out the door. Lisa didn't imagine calling home would be this painful. The walk to her tent felt like walking to her death. How was she going to make through these next few months without her son?

As promised, Garcia was waiting for Lisa at the beer tent. She agreed after some serious begging to accompany him to the desert night life. The so-called club was crowded. When they walked in, she could barely get through. The DJ was standing in front of a laptop hooked to two speakers. He held a microphone to his mouth, singing along with the music.

"Now this is just desperate," she said to herself.

"Hey, Roberts, I'm going to get a drink. You want something?" Garcia asked, walking toward the services bar.

"Soda please," she answered, dancing a little to the music.

Garcia returned with the drinks and Rottweiler in his company. Lisa wasn't too thrilled to see him.

"Check out those guys." Garcia pointed to the six men in battle dress.

"Yeah, we got a few marines here and there," Rottweiler screamed toward the direction of the men. "They're pretty cocky, so every now and then we have to put them in their place."

"Marines? I thought this was an air base?" Lisa asked, confused.

"Guess we thought wrong." Garcia laughed.

"You would think this was their base the way they strut around in their tight uniforms." Rottweiler shook his head.

"Now, Mr. Rottweiler, you seem like the kind of man who likes to start trouble. So let me warn you, if you get into something with one of them, don't expect my boy Garcia to jump in with you," she retorted while taking a sip of her soda.

He smiled. "Nope, not me. I'm a good boy."

"Yeah, okay." She turned her attention to Juan, who was dancing with an unknown woman. "I'm going outside," Lisa screamed just enough so he could hear her.

"You want me to come with you?" he asked.

She shook her head and then headed out the door. The starry sky almost hypnotized her as she watched each bright light swim in a sea of darkness. Nights like this were uncommon in a heavily polluted environment like Delaware. The air was the perfect temperature. She felt safe enough to be alone and decided a nice walk would help clear her mind. Dazed in her thoughts, she never noticed a man approaching her.

"Now why is a nice woman like you out here walking by herself?" he joked.

Lisa was far from the mood to have any company. "Clearing my head." Her face showed no sign of comfort. He was an older gentleman who looked like he could be her father or uncle.

"Let me guess, you just got here and you're feeling a little homesick?" he said.

"Something like that." She hoped her cold attitude would make him get the hint, but he just kept walking next to her.

"That's understandable. I left my wife and six-year-old son in Alabama to come here."

The idea of the man sharing the same feeling helped ease her mind a little. "Yeah, I just left my five-month-old. I'm still not used to it."

"Even after two months, it still doesn't get much better. You just have to find your own way of handling it."

She didn't want to entertain a conversation, but it was nice to vent to someone about her frustration. "Okay, how do you handle it?" she asked curiously.

"I try to avoid calling home." He smirked. "You see, men can't handle the separation, nor can we express ourselves like women. We bottle it up, poke our chest out, and try to roll with the punches."

"And that works, huh?" Not calling home seemed almost too easy. "You don't miss hearing their voices?"

"Of course I do, but sometimes when you overload your schedule and not think so much about it, you will notice the days will fly away." He waved in the sky. "By the way, everyone around here calls me Pops." He extended his hand.

"Okay, Pops, I'm Lisa." She returned his handshake with a smile.

"Lisa, why are you walking around by yourself?"

"I wanted to clear my mind away from all the music and the people. I don't get much time to think at work." She looked to the sky.

"Well, I'll leave you be. Remember, if you need anything, don't be afraid to call." He waved.

The old man had a point. As much as she didn't want to admit it, it was nice not to think about home. She never dreamed of being a mother nine months after joining the military, but there he was. Junior came into her life, changing her from a child to a woman. It was unfair to leave him at such an early age, but she had no choice. Her son needed her more than her country, but that was no longer her decision. If she was going to survive these next few months without losing her sanity, the best way to go was to pretend family life didn't exist. He was right. *I think I can wait out the phone calls for a little bit.*

CHAPTER 23

New Assignment

January 8, 2004

The sun was shining through a small opening of the tent. Whoever came in last must have forgotten to close it all the way. Monique stood up and walked slowly to the entrance. It was her day off, and the only thing she wanted to do was sleep. A shadow was making its way toward her. She figured it was one of her tent mates. Before she could pull the zipper all the way down, a hairy beast was making his way inside. Monique screamed to the top of her lungs, alerting all the other women who were grabbing their weapons and ducking for cover.

The monster pushed his way in, almost trampling Monique to the ground. She swung her fist while the others joined in.

"Stop, you guys, stop," screamed a voice in the background. The women pulled away from Fred, while Leslie turned on the lights.

"Are you serious? Who let Fred in here?" another voice said behind Monique.

"How was I supposed to know it was him? It's dark up in here, and all I saw was a shadow," Monique defended.

"All right, ladies, go back to bed. I'll take him out," said Leslie, grabbing on to Fred's ID badge. "Come on, boy, you know you're not supposed to be in here," she scolded the animal as if he could understand her.

Monique and the others were still out of breath. "How can any of us go back to bed after that?"

"Grant, you know you can be fined if you hurt a camel out here, right?" One of the girls in the crowd laughed.

"Funny," Monique responded sarcastically. "Now everybody knows if the Wing King finds out that beast is on this base, all of us is getting paperwork, right?"

Leslie walked back in, wiping her hands on her shorts. "Anybody up for breakfast?" she asked and smiled.

While the women were walking toward the chow hall, Monique could see Rogers running toward her.

"Hey, Mo, report at 0800," he said, catching his breath.

"On my day off? What's this about, Rog? I just got into a fistfight this morning; I'm really not up for anything but food and sleep," she explained.

"Fistfight? With who?" he asked, alarmed.

"You don't want to know. Let's just say it wasn't a fair fight." She frowned.

"Well get ready for the games, because Colonel Thomas wants us there eight a.m. sharp," he repeated and then ran back toward the opposite direction.

Monique did as told and headed back to change into her gear. She wasn't prepared for what he was going to tell them. Questions ran through her mind like the traffic in New York City. The problem was she wasn't sure if they were in trouble or if they were going to have to support another mission. After everything that happened on the last trip, she would have rather been in trouble then to hear her commander say she would have to travel off base.

Once she arrived at Colonel Thomas's office, Hernandez and Rogers were already standing at attention next to his door. She stood behind the other two, waiting patiently to be called.

"Bring them in," Monique heard Colonel Thomas command.

"Oh, goodness, here we go," Monique mumbled, marching behind Hernandez. They formed a line in front of Colonel Thomas's desk so he could get a good look at each one of them.

Rogers lifted his arm for a salute but was interrupted.

"At ease, you guys aren't in trouble." He stood up to look out the window. They stood in silence. "I bet you are all wondering why I asked you three to report to my office on your day off." Still no response. He turned around to look at the three troops who were still standing at attention. "You three have just volunteered for a special-duty assignment."

"Special duty, Sir?" Reyes asked.

"You all know we have contractors building the new Intelligence office. So the wing commander is asking for volunteers to . . ." He paused for a moment. "Well, there's no gentle way of putting this—he needs volunteers to babysit contractors." He smiled.

"When do we report, sir?" asked Monique, dreading the answer. The smirk on his face almost made her regret she even asked.

"Tomorrow, 0600. You'll report to the armory at 0530, gear up, and then proceed to the main gate."

There was no expression; they looked like zombies staring directly at the wall. Monique wasn't too thrilled with the idea of standing in over hundred-degree weather watching civilian men build buildings, but arguing with a colonel in a hazardous environment was definitely career suicide.

"Any questions?" Colonel Thomas asked while slowly scanning each member. There was no response. "Well, if that's all, you are dismissed," he commanded and then returned their salute. They marched out of his office in unison.

January 9, 2004

Monique stood in front of six men, shaking her head. She felt like a human waterfall. Her body was drenched in sweat from head to toe. Leslie stood next to her, taking slow sips out of her canteen.

"What the hell was I thinking walking into that recruiter's office?!" Monique screamed out in frustration. "It's hot, and I'm ready to shoot anything that moves for entertainment," she whined.

"Grant, it's not that bad." Leslie smiled while she faced the contractors hard at work. "Be glad you're not one of them." She pointed to the men who were covered in dirt, sand, and sweat.

"Yeah, I guess you're right." She looked around. A moving object caught her attention that almost looked unreal.

"Les, what is that?" Monique squealed, pointing to the scary-looking creature.

Leslie looked down, eyes wide. "That, my friend," she paused, "is a reason to fire your weapon!".

Monique ran in panic while Leslie laughed. The camel spider was almost the size of a grown man's hand. Its tan colored body and long arms made him look much more dangerous than he actually was. Rumors spread across the base of how a soldier fell asleep one evening and a camel spider bit his ear off. Monique refused to test that theory and instead decided to flee from it.

"Shoot it!" Monique continued to scream until she was next to Hernandez, who too was laughing.

"Calm down, Grant, it's just a baby." Hernandez laughed.

"That is not a baby! That is a monster!" Monique couldn't find the humor.

"You've been in the sun too long, my friend. Why don't you go to the shack and take a break?" Leslie tried to comfort her while waving her hands until the spider moved to the opposite direction.

"No, I'm good." She adjusted her desert uniform and walked back over to her post.

The Iraqi contractors laughed, making side jokes Monique couldn't understand.

"All right now, I wouldn't get too smart because this woman right here is American and she will shoot you," Monique screamed in the direction of the men.

"Monique it is not that serious," Leslie said.

Monique shook her head at the idea that women were forced to keep their place. Sometimes when they went off base, they were forced to follow the same rules. Do not talk to the men unless it was absolute necessary. After all, they would never take a female soldier seriously, so why argue? The image of the girl flashed through her mind. *I wonder why she was bleeding. Could I have helped her?* The idea of watching another woman in pain and feeling helpless almost made her feel useless. Her thoughts were broken as she and Hernandez were approached by Gabir.

"Good day," Gabir greeted in a thick Arabic accent. He was a translator from a nearby city.

"Hey, Gab." Hernandez jumped to shake his hands with a wide-eyed smile. "What's the deal?"

Gabir shook his head. As a child, his father had taught him English so that he could someday go to college and work as an engineer in the American country. After watching his father fall to the floor from a bullet wound to the chest, he continued to hold on to that dream. Working as a translator for the Americans paved a way for him to take care of his mother and two sisters. What his father never taught him was the language among the younger generation was a bit different from the typical English taught from a textbook. His puzzled look gave them the impression he had no idea what Hernandez was asking him.

"Gab, man, you gotta get with the language if you trynna roll with us," Rogers interrupted.

"What language? You mean Ebonics?" Monique shook her head. "The man just learned English, something you guys know nothing about." She laughed. "He could probably teach you two how to speak a bit more properly."

"Hold on, I speak proper English, Ebonics, and Spanish, Ms. Lady. I guess that makes me trilingual." Hernandez cupped his hands together. *"Un solo idioma nunca es suficiente."* He laughed.

"Dude, I understand you all multicultural and proud and everything. However, this is still America." Leslie paused for a moment while everyone looked at her. "Well, an American base."

"I learn basic English, which is good enough for me." Gabir smiled. "You young Americans are funny." He laughed.

The twinkle in his eyes was almost childlike. He was very well known around the base as a very likeable and respectable gentleman. As a translator, it was difficult for him to be seen with fellow soldiers in case any insurgents were watching him. It wasn't uncommon for translators or their families to be killed for aiding American troops. In several cases, a few of them were transferred to other countries once they retired to avoid any conflicts with the locals. Once you were considered a traitor, the life sentence was death. Making friends in his country was difficult, which gave him a lot of free time to spend with family.

The sun was out, and the temperature was high. They were all drenched in sweat while watching each contractor continue his duties. A loud man was screaming to the top of his lungs to one of the gate guards. Hernandez grabbed his weapon, heading toward the angry man and the woman standing next to him.

"Yo, Gab, go see what he wants," Hernandez said while Rogers followed quickly behind.

Gabir quickly ran toward the man speaking in the native language. *"Hal beemkani mosa'adatuk?"*

The man was speaking entirely too fast for anyone to even try to get an idea of what he was saying. Gabir raised his hand and shook his head.

The man screamed, pointing at the young girl. She was covered from head to toe, with only her dark, bloodshot eyes exposed.

"What is he saying?" asked Rogers.

"She needs a doctor," Gabir responded.

"For what?" Hernandez asked, scanning the woman from head to toe.

"Oh, no, she's in labor!" screamed Monique, running to the young girl. The gate guard soared in front of Gabir and the man, trying to explain he couldn't bring the girl on base. It was obvious even to a blind eye that she was in severe pain. Disregarding the seven security forces policemen surrounding the gate, Monique pushed past them and grabbed the girl before she hit the ground. Hernandez grabbed her arm, dragging her limp body into the police shack. There were screams coming from every direction, and it was almost impossible to understand anyone. The man tried to reach for his wife, but two men were standing in his way. Gabir explained what was going on, but he continued to fight his way in.

"Someone call for a medic. She's about to deliver." Monique attempted to remove the black veil that covered her face, but the woman grabbed her hand, glaring at Hernandez. It was obvious she wasn't allowed to show any part of her body to the strange man in the room.

"Hernandez, you can't be in here," Leslie screamed.

"This is no time to be bashful. She could be hemorrhaging," Hernandez argued.

"Please," Monique screamed. Hernandez stood for a moment and then turned his attention to the girl, who was breathing heavily. He slowly stood up and walked out the door.

Two other women entered the room with wet towels. Monique removed the veil from the young girl's face and rubbed the water against her forehead. This seemed to calm her down, which made it a little easier to attempt communication. She couldn't get over how beautiful and young the girl was.

"Now what?" asked Leslie as she eyed the girl.

"We need to control the bleeding," said Monique, rubbing the girl's head.

There was still yelling and screaming coming from the other side of the door.

"I wish they would shut up." Monique shook her head. The girl grabbed her stomach in pain as one of the other women tried to push her to lay flat on the floor. Leslie pulled her down while the others scrambled, trying to call for help. The young girl couldn't understand anything the American women were saying, and the pain was only getting worse.

"Listen, I know you are in pain, but you have to calm down," one of the soldiers said slowly, as if the girl could understand. The young woman grabbed her swollen belly, screaming to the top of her lungs.

"This is just great. We can't understand her and she can't understand us. The only translator we have is a male, and he's not allowed in here." Monique threw her hands up.

"That's not the only thing. Look at the left side of her head." One of the women pointed to the large blue and black bruise on her eye.

"Hold on, I learned a few things from the Intelligence briefing," said one of the women, pulling out a small black notebook from her flack vest. She turned through the pages until she found what she was looking for and then looked back at the girl. *"Ma esmouki?"*

Her eyes lit up. *"Esmee Saleema."*

"Anderson, what did you just say to her?" Leslie interrupted the conversation.

"Her name is Saleema." Anderson turned back to the Saleema and continued to attempt her Arabic. *"Hal tatakallamo alloghah al enjleziah?"*

"Qaleelan!" Saleema responded.

"Esmee Denise." Anderson pointed to herself. She pointed a finger to each one of the women in the room and introduced them accordingly. Saleema took it upon herself to try to say each one of the names to match the face.

"Is that your husband outside?" Anderson asked slowly.

Saleema nodded.

"Okay, can you understand me when I say we don't want to hurt you, we're sending help?" Anderson continued to speak slowly.

"Help," Saleema attempted in broken English.

"Just lay down and we'll take care of you, okay?" Anderson assured her.

Saleema's puzzled face told them she did not understand much of what she said.

"How old do you think she is?" Leslie asked.

"No more than sixteen or seventeen," Monique blurted.

The young girl collapsed, holding tightly to her belly. Leslie continued to rub her head with the wet towels.

"Monique, call medic again and find out what's taking them so long," Leslie ordered.

Monique rushed outside. The screaming man was on the ground at gunpoint. "What happened?" She looked over at Rogers.

"His family was killed in an attack. I guess he thinks it's unsafe to take his wife to the nearby hospital. When you guys grabbed her, he tried to attack one of our guys." Rogers shook his head. "From what I hear, the Colonel isn't too happy about the situation."

"Well the girl in there looks like she can be his daughter, and on top of that she has a black eye." Monique scowled. "Not sure where she got that from."

"Mo, cut it out. Do you have any idea how much trouble we're all in?"

Monique thought for a moment and then decided to calm down.

"What's up with medic?" She questioned watching the men interrogate the ambusher.

"Medic is not going to rush out here for her." Rogers shook his head.

"Man, what are we going to do? We can't just leave her in there bleeding."

He grabbed her chin. "Hey, calm down; it's going to be okay."

"You're right." Monique adjusted her uniform. "So . . ." She jumped from the loud boom coming from behind. "What the . . ." She screamed as flying images of light shot above her head. Everyone quickly fell to the ground for cover, while others scrambled inside neighboring buildings.

"Incoming!" screamed one of the security forces members. The next boom landed on the half-constructed building, blowing the scraps of metal in every direction. The contractors quickly ran for shelter.

Monique crawled into the shack for cover. Hernandez and Rogers grabbed their weapons, searching for where the firing was coming from.

"Grant, what's going on out there?" Leslie hollered over the loud noise. All of the women inside the shack were lined against the walls, trying to peek out the window.

"Either the Australians are having target practice or we're being attacked," Monique hollered back. "Your guess is as good as mine."

"Get out of the shack!" one of the men screamed from outside.

The women complied while grabbing Saleema and pulling her out the door. She screamed as she hunched over in pain. Hernandez grabbed her arm and pulled her into the vehicle closest to them.

"Grant, we got to get her to the hospital before we get hit," he yelled as he jumped behind the wheel.

"My weapon is still in the shack," Leslie screamed, turning back to retrieve her weapon.

"Go get it!" Monique climbed into the passenger side. Hernandez slowly drove onto the road, coming to a complete halt.

After five minutes, Leslie still had not come out of the building and the firing only continued. Security forces blocked all areas of the entrance in case of ambush. A few landmarks around the gate were in pieces from the blows. Men scrambled for cover while others lay on the hot sand, injured from shrapnel. "Why is it taking her so long?" Rogers inquired, becoming impatient. They could barely see the building as clouds of smoke covered the entire area.

"Rogers, go get her, man!" Hernandez called out.

Rogers grabbed his weapon and headed back in the direction of the gate.

"Incoming!" screamed an unknown man from off in the distance. The whistling sound in the air was loud indicating something was going to fall nearby. Within seconds debris and smoke was everywhere. Monique turned her head to avoid the pressure and vibration from the blow. She could see Rogers in midair, landing directly on his back.

"Rogers!" screamed Monique. She exited the vehicle and ran as fast as she could to her comrade, who was lying on the ground motionless. She fell to her knees, pulling his lifeless body onto her lap. He wasn't breathing. Her eyes filled with water as she tried to compose herself. "Rogers, please wake up." She rocked him back and forth. Each tear from her eyes landed on his soiled face. His eyes were wide open, daydreaming into the clouds. Monique lifted his head slowly and kissed the middle of his forehead. She rubbed the blood and sweat residue from her lips fighting back the urge to cry louder.

Hernandez jumped to his feet, running toward the smoky building "Leslie?" He looked around, hoping to catch a glimpse of her body. There was no way in or out. *Leslie could not have survived this*. He turned back to check on Monique. He had already forgotten about the pregnant woman in the humvee. Monique barely moved while she stared into the dead man's eyes. He slowly walked behind, squatting down, placing both hands on her shoulders.

"He's gone, Grant," Hernandez spoke calmly.

All the chaotic noises around them were almost nonexistent in Monique's ears. Silence filled the air as she thought about Rogers. Her body was numb from the fear and the pain of losing her friends.

"No, he's just asleep, he'll wake up in a minute" she continued rocking him in her arms. He had no pulse and or life left in his body. Hernandez shook his head in disbelief. One minute Rogers was alive and the next he was gone.

"Somebody please help me!" a scream cried out to no one in particular. Monique popped her head up at the sound of Leslie's voice. She laid the upper half of Rogers's body back on the ground and then hopped to her feet.

"Leslie!" Monique sounded hopeful, following the sounds of the shaky voice. "Where are you?" She searched through the rubble until she noticed a hand attempting to squeeze through the tiny opening.

"Here." She waved under piles of debris. Her cough was raspy from swallowing large amounts of dust. "Help me." She pushed the rubble off of her. Hernandez examined her before assisting her off the ground.

"Your legs are broken, Leslie," Hernandez said while moving chunks of glass from her open wound.

"Oh, is that why I can't feel them?" she asked sarcastically.

Monique and Hernandez dragged her to the vehicle where Saleema was. She was crying and hunched over from the labor pains. Afraid and alone she wondered what had happened to her husband. *Was he dead?* The visual of the injured American woman covered in blood frightened the young girl. Monique hopped back into the passenger side while Hernandez took control of the vehicle.

CHAPTER 24

Trouble on the Home Front

February 26, 2004

*I*t had been almost two months since Lisa called home. The idea of running from her pain and heartache helped eased her nerves. She prepared for work just in time for the morning rush. Every morning she fought off eighty women for a pointless three- to five-minute shower. She prayed for an off schedule so she could avoid all the unnecessary morning drama. The first moment she walked through the door, tragedy was already in the air, from the young women clustered together to discuss who said what to the men bragging about who got to "her" first. Lisa shook her head at all the nonsense. Sometimes it was just best to stay to herself. She maneuvered throughout the warehouse to a nearby desk. Sand covered every inch of the computer, making it almost a habit to brush before use. Lisa noticed the stacks of labels sitting nearby. She figured they were customer orders that needed to be pulled. Before tending to her duties, she logged onto the computer to check her e-mail. Anita sent three messages within a ten-minute time period to call, and there were a few messages from her bank. As she scrolled over the website, her balance read zero.

"Huh?" she blurted, grabbing the phone and dialing home, but there was no answer. Lisa sat frustrated, unable to figure why her account was empty. The only one who had access to it was Brian. "Why would this fool take all of my money?" The math wasn't adding up. The money she received was tax free, plus a few incentives for family separation. She blew out a deep breath, dialing her office number.

"Storage and issue, unsecured line. May I help you, sir or ma'am?" the voice answered in a proper tone.

"Jasmine, what's going on? Nita there?" Lisa asked anxiously.

"Nope, but you got some explaining to do, ma'am," Jasmine responded sternly.

"And why is that?"

"Why didn't you tell me you were getting a divorce?"

Lisa was quiet for a moment. She couldn't figure out where Jasmine or Anita got that idea.

"Jasmine, what are you talking about?" Lisa questioned. "I haven't even spoken to Brian in a while, and the last time we spoke we were fine."

"When exactly was the last time you spoke to him?" Jasmine interrogated.

"Don't judge me, Jasmine, you have no idea how much it hurts to be away from Junior. I can't keep calling home and hearing him cry for his mother. It tears me up to the point I just want to run away from here." Lisa tried to hold back tears.

"First off, I'm not trying to judge you. What I'm trying to tell you is that while you are over there playing hide and seek, Brian has been here seeing someone else."

Lisa couldn't bring herself to say anything.

"Lisa, I thought you knew."

"You thought I knew that my husband was having an affair while I was a half a world away?" Lisa asked as calmly as she could. The last thing she wanted to do was take her frustration out on her best friend.

"I know things look bad right now, but you need to call Brian and find out what's going on. Maybe it's a big misunderstanding." The phone was silent for a few moments. Jasmine attempted to speak again. "Or maybe he was just lonely and needed some attention. It's obvious you weren't giving it to him."

Lisa wiped the tear flowing down her cheek away from sight. She hung up the phone without warning. Thoughts of calling Brian battled within her mind. If she called him, would he be honest, or would he try to continue to play as if everything was still good between them? No matter what, she needed to get to the bottom of the situation. When the operator connected the call, Brian picked up on the second ring.

"Hello," Brian said calmly. He sounded happy with his little boy in the background making noises. The sound of his voice made her regret deploying. She prayed Jasmine was lying or made a mistake.

"Hey, Brian, how are you?" Lisa spoke casually.

"What's up?" There was no sign of warmth in Brian's voice. It was hard to read if he was angry or happy.

"I checked my account today, and for some reason my balance is zero." She tried not to yell into the phone. The last thing she needed was the gossip squad spreading rumors her husband was spending all of her hard-earned money.

He blew out a long breath of frustration. "I had a few bills that needed to be paid. Is there a problem?"

"Brian, there was almost five grand in the account. What bills were you paying that caused you to steal all of my money?" she blurted.

"Your money, huh?" He laughed. "Well looks like when you signed that marriage contract, you agreed for it to be our money."

"You better not be spending money on that tramp you've been catering to around base."

"Look, I'm not in the mood to play games with you. If you want to believe rumors, then fine with me. I told you what I did with that money."

"Wow." Lisa was speechless. "Brian, it's not like that. I—"

"You want to speak to him? Because I sure as hell don't have anything to say to you," Brian interrupted. Before she could respond, Brian was already placing the phone to Junior's ear. "Come on, little man, it's your mommy. Say, 'I love you, Mommy.'"

"Hey, mommy's boy, I miss you," Lisa said cheerfully. She could tell Brian was playing with him so he would make noises over the phone. When the noises stopped, Brian put the phone back to his ear.

"Try to call more often. As much as it hurts you, he still has the right to talk to his mother," she heard Brian say before hanging up the phone.

"Hello?" The phone went dead.

"If you'd like to make a call, please hang up—" She hung up before the recording could instruct her to do another thing.

"Hey, Roberts, can you pull that stuff out of the warehouse? I'm about to make a run." Garcia interrupted her train of thoughts.

"Huh?" She jumped.

"You good? I asked could you pull these?" he asked, lifting the stack of labels. "You look like you're ready to murder someone."

She laughed in spite of her embarrassment. "No. I'm okay. I'll get that stuff ready." After taking a few moments to herself, she called her bank and suspended her account. "Let's see how far he gets now." She grabbed the labels and proceeded to the warehouse.

CHAPTER 25

Gone but Not Forgotten

March 3, 2004

onique rested her head on the pillow, hoping to ease her tension headache. The loud booms were becoming persistent. Since the attack days before, the insurgents were on pursuit. While the army armed the perimeter of the base, the support units were forced to remain within the gate at all times.

"Hey, you almost ready?" Hernandez walked through the doorway of her tent.

"When is this crap going to end? I hear it all day and all night," she whined, referring to the bombings.

"I hope soon. I can't even stand walking outside my tent without fearing something is going to hit this way." He sighed.

"So they decided to have the memorial after all?" she questioned.

"Yeah, I guess they feel we should be immune to the sounds of gunfire by now."

Monique tried to crack a smile but couldn't bring herself to do it. She slowly lifted from her bed and walked over to her chair.

"I'll be outside waiting for you," Hernandez said, slowly walking out. He turned back for a quick moment. "You know, Rogers was like my best friend. I'm sure going to miss him."

Monique nodded.

Monique slid through the tent doors to meet Hernandez, neither said a word. The crowd of airmen, soldiers, marines, and sailors was a reminder of the chaos that surrounded the place they temporarily called home. No one spoke as each party split into formation in front of their comrade's boots, rifle, and helmet arranged into the soldier's cross. The colors were posted, and the national anthem was sung. Once the invocation was said, a few individuals fell to one knee while others fought back tears. Others attempted to maintain military bearing but were unable to keep their composure. The commander waited for a moment and then proceeded to speak to the large mixed crowd.

The tall, proud army general stood before the sea of armed forces members. Their faces held no expression. Many were crying, while others were angry. He stood in front of the podium and then cleared his throat.

"Many of you came here today to mourn the fallen before me. Please know they did not die in vain. Their memory lives on in you. Do not forget, we came here to complete a mission. The men and women here paid a heavy price to perform that duty. When you leave here today, take them with you. Keep them in your prayers. Their families will be notified within the next few days. Pray for them as well—sons, daughters, mothers, fathers, all mourning for their loved ones. Many of you will leave here and go back to your normal lives; others are not so fortunate. If you don't believe in something, you may want to start today. God knows you'll need it." He stepped away from the podium, fighting back the urge to say more. Less was best at the moment.

The crowd was silent while the chaplain stood in front of them and read a few Scriptures in his Bible. Once he was finished, he closed the pages and waved it in the air. "If you do not believe in this Bible, find something within yourself to get you through these next few hours."

Monique's legs were weak from standing. Hernandez barely moved as roll call began. The general called each name of the fallen.

"Staff Sergeant . . . Airman First Class . . . Specialist . . ."

None of the names registered in their brains. They waited and anticipated one name that would forever stay in their memories.

"Staff Sergeant Anthony Rogers."

Monique could hear her heart pounding in her ears. She prayed it was a mistake many times after the explosion. The reality was her best friend was gone. As "Taps" played, Hernandez and Monique stood silent and motionless. Members slowly formed a line in front of each memorial, paying their last respects. Monique walked over to the statue that represented Rogers. She rubbed his dog tags and closed her eyes tightly. She thought back to his laugh, his touch and smell. Her tears burned like acid. The soldier's cross confirmed Rogers was never coming back. After what seemed like eternity, both managed to turn away from the view of their friend's belongings.

"That wasn't so bad," Monique lied as the two began walking in the opposite direction.

"Yeah, I guess," Hernandez uttered. He looked up and saw Leslie rolling toward them in her wheelchair.

"Wow, don't you look like crap," Monique joked.

"I still look better than you, broken legs and all." Leslie laughed.

"Yeah," Monique responded while trying to hold back the urge to cry.

"Looks like you're on your way out this weekend," Hernandez intervened.

"Yeah, just my luck I couldn't get hurt in the middle of my tour. They waited until it was almost time for me to go home." Leslie sucked her teeth.

"I thought injured folks get sent to Ramstein?" Hernandez questioned.

"Unfortunately, flights were delayed. I'll be leaving soon. At least I get to go home a week early. I know my little boy misses me." She smiled, trying to brighten the mood.

"Just remember to keep in touch. I'll be home soon," Monique continued.

"You got it." Leslie extended her arms to hug Monique.

CHAPTER 26

Home Sweet Home

April 30, 2004

The first moment Lisa stepped off of the plane, she took one deep breath of the Baltimore air and exhaled as long as she could. After what seemed like an eternity, she was finally home. She could not wait until she saw Junior. The long line to customs was almost out the gate. It did not matter as long as she was on American soil. The young inspector directed her to the nearest table to empty all of her belongings. The man with the white beard and big build examined each item carefully after reviewing her card.

"Anything else in your pockets?" he asked sternly.

"No, sir, just lint." She laughed. The man did not return a smile.

It didn't matter, just as long as she walked through the double doors to be greeted by her baby boy. The carrier on luggage she was toting around began to get heavy. As the doors opened, Jasmine and Anita were standing in front of her with a sad look on their faces.

"Hey, ladies, where's my baby?" Lisa asked excitedly.

"Brian has him," Jasmine responded in a low tone.

"Okay, what's going on?" Lisa asked, crossing her arms.

"Let's get your things and head to the car," Jasmine said.

"No, one of you is going to tell me what's going on. Something is up, and I can feel it, so what gives?" Lisa asked, irritated.

"Lisa, this is not the time or the place to have this discussion," Anita whispered.

"Please." Lisa crossed her arms.

"Brian moved out," Anita responded. Both women looked at each other, turning back to Lisa.

"Why?" Lisa asked suspiciously.

"He moved in with his fiancée," Anita continued.

Lisa was stunned. "Fiancée? How do you have a fiancée when you're supposed to be married?" she yelled, attracting unwanted attention.

Anita looked around at all the people staring at the volatile woman.

"Look, Lisa, can we finish this discussion in the car?" Anita begged.

Lisa couldn't respond. She nodded as she walked toward the baggage claim. As they grabbed her mobility bags and headed for the car, no one said a word. They all huddled inside the car, snapping their seatbelts one by one. Anita reached into her purse and grabbed what looked to be a camera and folded paper. She handed the paper to Lisa without making eye contact. Lisa unfolded the paper and read the content.

When she finished reading, her red eyes darted to Anita, who was trying not to make eye contact. "Anita, did you just serve me?" Lisa panicked.

"I didn't want to do it, but if anybody was going to break this news to you, I'd rather it had been me," Anita argued. "Brian was going to have a lawyer do it."

Lisa voice cracked as she attempted to speak. "But why?"

Anita handed the camera to Lisa, exposing pictures of Brian with another woman. The woman in the photos looked familiar.

"Who is this?" Lisa asked. One of the pictures was of Brian, Junior, and the woman at the park. "And why is she with my son?"

"Her name is Amanda. Apparently Brian and this woman have had an ongoing relationship for over a year," Jasmine said.

"She was the one he was seeing before Junior was born?" Lisa shut her eyes, thinking back to the day of the barbecue.

"Yeah," Anita replied. "Please believe me when I tell you he caught hell for this."

"I can't believe this." Lisa shook her head. "They kept a relationship the entire time." Unable to see anymore, she threw the camera back to Anita. "Take me home."

"You don't want to get Junior?" Jasmine asked.

"If I see Brian right now, I will shoot him." Her face was serious.

The drive to Dillan was long. None of the women had anything to say to each other. What should have been a joyous occasion was more of a dramatic ending. After the conversation with Brian, Lisa made it a point to avoid calling home. The last thing she needed was to argue with him over petty nonsense. What she didn't realize was the distance was only pushing Brian away even further into Amanda's arms. She fought off the urge to cry. Enough was enough. As Anita pulled up to the house, Lisa grabbed her bags and headed inside. The ladies remained in the car. As she flicked on the lights, a sudden burst of rage consumed her like an animal ready for attack. All the furniture was new and looked expensive. The picture frames on the wall showed photos of the once-happy family. If she had a lighter and gasoline, she would have set fire to the memories. Instead she picked up a nearby baseball bat that was used to fend off potential predators. In one quick swing, Lisa hit each picture frame one by one until glass scattered on the floor. The coffee table in the middle of the floor was next. She hit the glass surface, smashing it into pieces. When that didn't ease the pain, she walked over to the CD player and hit the top as hard as she could. The plastic split in two, falling to the floor. She scanned the room for something else to take her frustration out on.

"You bastard!" she screamed while swinging at the lamp sitting peacefully on the table stand. "This is what you spent my money on!"

As she swung to hit the computer sitting on the desk in the corner, Jasmine ran over to her, grabbing the bat while in the air. "Lisa, don't do this!"

Lisa glared at Jasmine.

"I know you're hurt, but this isn't the answer," she pleaded while looking at the mess.

Lisa was out of breath and bleeding from cutting her hand on the glass. She looked like a mad woman.

"He betrayed me and spent all my money!" Lisa yelled, still out of breath. "On this expensive stuff and that woman he's parading around my son!"

"And destroying everything made you feel better?" Jasmine shook her head.

"No, it brought me justice!" Lisa blurted.

"Lisa, please, let's get you to the hospital."

"No, I'm not done!" she yelled, looking at the new computer sitting on the desk.

"How are you going to destroy everything now? I'm not giving this back to you." Jasmine waved the bat in front of her.

"Fine, you want to take my bat from me; I'll do it with my hands!" she said, knocking the computer off of the desk. "I gave him a baby that wasn't even his!"

"Lisa, stop!" Jasmine pulled her away from the corner, causing her to lose her balance. She hit the floor, sliding toward where the coffee table once stood.

Lisa paused for a moment, still out of breath. She examined her reflection in the broken pieces of glass on the floor. Her face was red and her hair was out of place. Blood dripped to the floor from the cuts in her hand.

"How about you leave my house," Lisa said calmly as she slowly lifted off of the floor. "I have to clean this mess up."

"No, I'll have someone come by and clean up. I don't want you here right now. You are in no condition to stay here alone."

Lisa was far from in the mood to argue with anyone. What she thought would help only caused her more heartache. The entire living room was a wreck. Pictures were hanging off of the wall. She picked up the family portrait from the ground. The smiling faces were a reminder her family was gone.

"Oh, God," she cried as she slouched to the floor. Her hands hit the floor, cutting them again on the glass. "How could he do this to me?"

Jasmine tiptoed over to Lisa, trying to avoid stepping on shards of glass. She grabbed Lisa's arms, lifting her up. "Lisa, I love you, but you have to pull yourself together. He's not worth this. We will help you get through this, I promise you." She embraced her with a strong hug.

CHAPTER 27

The Courtroom

November 17, 2004

"*M*s. Roberts, did you have anything you would like to say?" the judge asked Lisa, breaking her out of a daze.

"Huh?" she asked, startled. Her lawyer nudged her arms. "Oh." She stood to her feet and walked toward the podium. She avoided eye contact with Brian.

"Your Honor, I brought Jerry Owens here today, along with a paternity test, to show that he is the biological father. I feel it's only right that he is given a chance for custody." She handed the papers to the bailiff, who then placed them in front of the judge.

Lisa turned to face Brian, whose facial expression was cold. He grasped the seat with a tight grip to avoid leaping in her direction. If he could touch her, he probably would have beaten her. Jerry smiled while the judge reviewed each piece of paper on his desk.

"I'll review the evidence presented today and determine how we will handle this situation," the judge responded. "As of right now, both parties agree the divorce is final. Mr. Roberts, you will keep all of the household goods, while you, Ms. Roberts, will walk out of my courtroom with absolutely nothing?" he reassured. "Is that correct?"

"Yes, sir. I just want to make everything right. I know I hurt a lot of people, but it's the right thing to do," she continued.

"In that case, Ms. Roberts, I will not penalize you for the damaged property." The judge looked over to Brian, who was sitting quietly. "Mr. Roberts, do you have anything you would like to add?"

"No, sir," he replied through clenched teeth.

"The court will proceed at a later date in regard to custody. At this time, the child will remain with the mother until a future decision is made. The divorce has been granted," he said, dismissing the courtroom.

Brian stood up, charging toward Lisa. "So you want to play hardball with my son, huh?"

"Mr. Roberts either you calm down or we'll take you into custody," the security guard yelled from across the room.

Lisa smiled at Brian with an evil grin. "At this point, Brian, there is no way you could hurt me anymore than you already have."

"If you were a man, I would punch you right in the jaw," he whispered.

"Is that a threat, Mr. Roberts?" Lisa's lawyer asked.

"Better not be," said Jerry as he stood up, face to face with Brian. "You need to get out of her face."

Brian glared at Jerry.

"No, it's okay Jerry." She stood facing the man she once loved. "First off, Junior is Jerry's biological son. And he has every right in the world to step in and be his father. I'm the one who made this mess, and I will not let my son pay for my mistakes, even if that risks you hating me."

"Once I get my son back, I will be changing his name," Jerry interrupted.

"He's my son. You better remember that," Brian argued.

"Do what you have to do." Lisa grabbed her belongings and headed out the door. The only thing that mattered at that moment was getting to her car. Both men stood behind her, watching her walk through the door. The two men she once loved and gave her all for were now in her past. It was time to move on.

After putting her mind at ease, reminiscing on past loves and experience, her thoughts were interrupted by the vibration of her phone. She flipped it open.

"Yes, ma'am," she answered.

"Lisa?"

"Gerard?" Lisa asked. "Why are you calling me from Monique's phone?"

"I guess you haven't heard," he said, disappointed.

"Heard what?"

"Monique crashed her car into a tree."

"What?" Lisa panicked. "Is she okay?"

"She's okay now. Apparently she was drunk."

"But Mo doesn't drink." Lisa was confused.

"She did last night. According to her friends here at the base, she's been out every night since she came home." Gerard growled. "One of her friends called me last night, so I caught a last-minute flight. Your girl owes me seven hundred dollars."

"Okay, well let me get Junior and I'll be on my way down." Lisa closed her phone.

CHAPTER 28

Hospital Visit

November 22, 2004

Monique's eyes fluttered open. The pounding in her head made her flinch in pain. "Oh, God, make the room stop spinning," she cried. When she finally focused her eyes, Gerard was standing over her with a disappointed look. She looked around the room at all of the hospital equipment. There were IVs coming from every direction. Her head was heavy, and her muscles ached.

"Gerard, what happened to me?" She examined the tubes coming out of her arms.

"Mo, you were in an accident. Your car is totaled, but luckily you came out okay." He shook his head.

"I don't get it," she said groggily.

"Mo, you were drunk. Your blood level was beyond illegal. I'm surprised they didn't just take you to jail." He laughed.

"Jail?" she shook her head, trying to remember the final moments before she fell into a temporary coma.

"Why didn't you tell me you had a problem?" he scolded.

"What are you talking about? I don't have a problem," she denied.

"Oh, really? Monique, you don't even drink. And then you wrap your car around a tree on a suicide mission." He stood up and paced back and forth. "I got a phone call from someone who lived in your dorms."

Monique didn't say a word.

"What if you'd been killed? How would I have known?"

"I'm sorry," she managed to say.

"That's all you can say to me?" He scowled at her.

"What do you want me to say?' she yelled.

"Tell me why."

How could she explain to the man she loved her depression spiraled from losing her best male friend? Gerard was a good man but nonetheless a jealous one. If he even had the slightest clue Monique was sad over another man, he would end the relationship fast.

"I've been through a lot these last few months," she lied.

Gerard threw his hands in the air. "Why didn't you call me?" He shook his head and then paused for a moment. "Did you love him?"

The question startled her. "What?"

"It's a simple question, really. Did you love him that much you would rather drink your sorrows away than to come to me and I could help you work through this?"

"Gerard, what are you talking about?"

"You know what I'm talking about," he snapped.

"No, I didn't. He was my friend. That's it."

Gerard covered his face with his hands. "This was my fault," he said, turning to face her.

"What are you talking about?"

Gerard pulled his chair next to her hospital bed. "I've been dragging you through this long-distance relationship for almost two years. I should've known I couldn't keep doing this to you."

"Gerard, what are you saying? You want to break up or something?" Monique stared at him.

He slowly pulled something out of his pocket. "Mo, I love you. And if I'm going to hold on to you, you need a commitment from me." He exposed the band in his hand.

"What is that, Gerard?" she asked, aggravated.

"Marry me."

Monique was shocked. She never thought Gerard gave marriage a second thought. They'd been back and forth with the long-distance relationship for so long, it was almost normal.

"Just like that? You don't want to know anything about Rogers? You don't have any insecure feelings? I mess up and you want to marry me?" Monique's thoughts were going a mile a minute.

"A Leslie called you. I answered your phone because, yes, I'm insecure, and I thought it was another man. When I told her what happened to you, she went on about the explosion and Rogers." He stared at her, waiting for her response, but she couldn't speak. "I know nothing happened. I'm just hurt you didn't come to me."

Monique looked around the room and then focused back on Gerard. "So you're not mad?"

"No, because I love you and I just want you with me. So will you marry me?"

"On one condition." She looked down at her hands.

"What is it?" He raised his eyebrows.

"I want two kids."

Gerard smiled. "That's it?"

"And a puppy," she continued, playing with her fingers.

"Deal." He smiled, grabbing her face and kissing her on the forehead.

November 23, 2004

Lisa walked into the room where Monique rested. She slowly crept to the side of her bed and placed her hand gently on Monique's forehead. She jumped at the cold hands pressed against her skin and then smiled at her best friend.

"Hey, kiddo." Lisa smiled.

"Hey," Monique said groggily.

"You really got yourself into it this time, didn't you?" Lisa examined her from head to toe.

"What are you talking about? I'm fine." She adjusted herself so she was sitting up straight.

"Why didn't you tell me?" Lisa sighed. "You could have killed yourself."

"Now you sound like Gerard. He already put me through this lecture." She smiled slightly.

"Mo, how could you be so stupid? Why didn't you just call me and tell me you were going through something? I would've been here for you." Lisa paced back and forth.

Monique didn't say a word.

"Out of everyone in this world, you are the only one who I can truly call family. What if I lost you?"

"Now you know you can't get rid of me that easily." She laughed.

Lisa slipped in the bed next to Monique and placed her head on her shoulder.

"What happened?" Lisa asked softly.

"I don't know. One minute I was fine and then the next all I could feel was rage. Lisa, I got off that plane and everyone around me was walking around carrying on with their daily lives. It was like they just don't care anymore about what goes on over there. It hurt." Monique wiped her eyes, refusing to cry.

"I know. People are tired of the war. As long as they don't see it, they don't care."

"All I remember was going from bar to bar with some people from the base. We were so drunk, and I could not remember for the life of me where I left my car." She thought back to the night before the accident. "It took twenty minutes, but I finally found it. I got in, drove from one traffic light to another, and next thing I knew, I woke up to some medic sticking needles in my arm."

"What's the damage?"

"Aside from a DUI on my record, a suspended license, possible demotion, and thirty-day confinement to the base, ah not much really." She waved her hand in the air.

"Glad you're keeping a positive attitude about this." Lisa shook her head.

"Got to laugh to keep from crying, right?" Monique adjusted the IV resting on her left arm. "The commander said if I go to mental health and get into their program, they will lessen the charges."

"Doesn't seem like a bad idea."

"Where's my nephew?" Monique asked, changing the subject.

"Outside with Gerard."

"So how did the divorce go? I know for a fact Brian flipped his head when he saw Jerry walk in that courtroom."

Lisa slowly nodded. "Yep, he did. You know it took me four weeks to make that phone call after Jasmine and Nita served me the divorce papers." She blew out a deep breath, staring into the ceiling. The pain was still fresh. "I know he thinks I did it to be vindictive, but what was I supposed to do?"

Monique thought to herself for a moment. "It was a hard call. I know we weren't there for you like we should've been. We gave you some really bad advice."

"No, you didn't. You were just looking out for me."

"How does Jerry feel about all this? Is he going to fight you for custody?"

"Nope. We go back to court later, and the judge will decide. I gave him all the supporting documents needed, and Jerry took his paternity test. In the meantime, Junior is in my custody."

"Girl, you stay getting yourself in sticky situations," Monique blurted out, laughing.

"Yeah, and last time I checked I had some help." Lisa shoved Monique in the arm.

"Regardless, I'm glad you finally allowed Jerry into his life. I could see Junior resenting you for it in the future."

Lisa sighed. "Yeah, I know. I thought I was doing what was best for my family. No baby's mother and father drama." She rolled her eyes.

"You know Jerry wants you back, right?" Monique grinned.

"Not going to happen." Lisa shook her head. "Enough of all that. What's this I hear about you, ma'am?"

"Oh, he told you?"

"Yeah, he did. Congrats are in order." Lisa grabbed her hand. "So when are we planning your engagement party?"

"The same time we plan your divorce party." Monique laughed.

"Of course. It will be a big hit. I say we invite every fed-up, scorned military female who was forced to endure playing superhero by day and fool by night." Lisa smiled.

"Man, you are not lying. It's hard trying to play so many roles, because in the end you will eventually fail on one if you don't plan and strategize accordingly." Monique reminisced back to Rogers. "But, Lis, can I ask you something?"

"What?"

"If you could go back and do it all over again, would you?"

Lisa thought for a moment and then looked at her best friend, grinning from ear to ear. "I sure would!"

Both girls laughed.

The bond formed between the two was proven over time to be unbreakable. The love of the sisterhood within the military was the only thing that kept them going. Both women faced their own obstacles but managed to overcome with the help of each other. In the male-dominated environment, women are bound together, encourage each other, and fight for one another.